THE NIGHT JOURNEY
Kathryn Kasky

Rachel dreads the afternoons she spends keeping her great-grand-mother company. Their conversations are tedious and time goes slowly—until Nana Sashie begins to reminisce about her child-hood in Russia. Slowly the events and characters of her past come to life, becoming as real to Rachel as members of her own family. But Rachel's parents think Nana Sashie should not be troubled with such thoughts, and so Rachel begins to go secretly to Nana Sashie's bedroom late at night. There she listens as the old woman spins her tale of a distant time, when Jews were forced to serve in the czar's army or were murdered in pogroms, a time when nine-year-old Sashie devised a wonderful plan for her family's escape…

THE
NIGHT
JOURNEY

❖❖❖❖❖❖❖❖❖❖❖❖❖❖❖

Kathryn Lasky

WITH DRAWINGS BY
Trina Schart Hyman

PUFFIN BOOKS

PUFFIN BOOKS
Published by the Penguin Group
Viking Penguin Inc., 40 West 23rd Street, New York, New York 10010, U.S.A.
Penguin Books Ltd, 27 Wrights Lane, London W8 5TZ England
Penguin Books Australia Ltd, Ringwood, Victoria, Australia
Penguin Books Canada Ltd, 2801 John Street, Markham, Ontario, Canada L3R 1B4
Penguin Books (N.Z.) Ltd, 182–190 Wairau Road, Auckland 10, New Zealand

Penguin Books Ltd, Registered Offices: Harmondsworth, Middlesex, England

First Published by Frederick Warne & Co., Inc., 1981
Published in Puffin Books 1986
Reprinted 1987 (twice), 1988

Printed in U.S.A.
by R. R. Donnelley & Sons Company, Harrisonburg, Virginia

Library of Congress Cataloging in Publication Data
Lasky, Kathryn.   The night journey.
Summary: A young girl ignores her parents' wishes and persuades
her great-grandmother to relate the story of her escape from czarist Russia.
[1. Jews—Soviet Union—Fiction.   2. Soviet Union—
History—Nicholas II, 1894–1917—Fiction]   I. Title.
PZ7.L3274Ni   1986   [Fic]   85-72097   ISBN 0-14-032048-2

FOR ANN LASKY SMITH,
who remembers

No savior from without can come
To those that live and are enslaved.
Their own messiah they must be,
And play the savior and the saved.

—SIMEON SAMUEL FRUG

THE NIGHT JOURNEY

❖ ❖ ❖ ❖ ❖ ❖ ❖   I   ❖ ❖ ❖ ❖ ❖ ❖ ❖

"CAN I touch your cheek, Nana Sashie?"

"As long as your fingers aren't smeared with candy—in that case put them in my mouth." She laughed, and Rache's fingers traced lightly over the plump soft cheeks. Nana Sashie's face reminded Rache of a big oiled potato, the pale smooth kind. There were some brown speckles, "age marks," her mother had said, but no wrinkles on her great-grandmother's face. "I'm too old for wrinkles," Nana Sashie had once told her when Rache asked why she didn't have any. "I've outgrown them," she added with a half snort, half giggle.

"But Nana Rose has them and she's old," Rache had countered.

"She's young old," Nana Sashie had answered.

"She's seventy!"

"That's young old," Nana Sashie had said. "I'm old old. Your skin gets like a baby's again when you're old old." And old old eyes must fade, Rache thought as she touched the smooth

1

cheeks and studied the face, for Nana Sashie's eyes were so pale that you could hardly guess what color they had ever been.

"Your face might look like a baby's, but it feels like a nice potato."

"Peeled or unpeeled?" Nana Sashie laughed hard at her own joke and rocked her rocker.

As long as Rache could remember, her great-grandmother Sashie had sat in this rocker wrapped up in a blizzard of fuzzy blankets and shawls. Every evening Rache's mom and dad carried Nana Sashie from the rocker downstairs to dinner and then back up to bed. In the morning they lifted her from the bed to the rocker again. Rache couldn't imagine anything worse or more boring than spending your life in a rocking chair.

Sometimes Nana Sashie was grouchy, and sometimes she would get confused and forget where she was and begin to speak in Russian and Yiddish, but the scariest for Rache was when Nana would begin to call her, Rache, "Mama." When this happened Rache, holding Nana Sashie's hand tightly, would yell for her own mother or father to come quick! One or both parents would come running, and after much cuddling of Nana Sashie and soft words, mostly "There there's" and "We're here's," Nana Sashie would calm down and soon be herself again. If someone had told her that she had called "Mama" three minutes before, she would have laughed at the notion. It was all part of being very old—old old. At least that was what Rache was told.

Rache was told a lot of things by her parents and her young old grandmother, Nana Rose, about what to do and not to do about Nana Sashie: don't talk to her about Great-grandpa, who had been a violinist and conductor; it makes her cry. And there had recently been a ban on playing his records in the house; the music not only made her cry but raised her blood pressure. Don't give her candy; she's a borderline diabetic. Do talk about the weather; it makes Nana Sashie warm and cozy to hear about wind-chill factors and icy roads when she's safe in her rocking chair. Do talk about your schoolwork—"Nana Sashie enjoys hearing about your schoolwork, dear." Do talk about your friends. Do talk about your secret club; she'll be "intrigued." The last "do" infuriated Rache on two counts: first, the secret club was last year, when she was twelve, and second, if you have a secret club, the point is *not* to talk about it.

Secret clubs aside, Rache was supposed to spend some time talking to Nana Sashie every afternoon, and this could be trying. Next to sitting in a rocking chair all day long, Rache could imagine nothing more boring than talking about her schoolwork. She had been declared "unmotivated," an "underachiever." Her report card showed straight B's. It even sounded dull. "Straight A's" had a ring to it. "All D's" had an earthy thud, but "Straight B's"? As far as her friends went, there was nothing to talk about. She had just had a fight with her best friend.

"Peeled," Rache said after a long pause. "Yes, a peeled Idaho." Rache sat back with a sigh and looked at Nana Sashie.

Nana Sashie stared at her with her pale eyes. "You're wondering how I sit here all day long in this rocker, no?" The question totally surprised Rache.

"No! No! I mean . . ."

"Yes, you are. It's hard for you to come up here and make

talky-talky"—she fluttered her hands a bit—"with an old lady."

"Oh, no, Nana Sashie! No! No!" Rache cried.

"Be quiet!" she said in a grouchy voice. "I'll tell you how I do it, how I sit here all day long, year after year. I remember. I remember all sorts of things." Then the old lady leaned out from the mohair storm that swirled around her and took Rache's hand so tightly that it almost hurt. "But Rachel, I am so old that I am beginning to forget, and that scares me." She squeezed her eyes shut until they were little lashless slits. A tear sprang out of a corner of each eye.

"Nana, it's not good for you to think about that stuff. It makes you sad." Rache thought of the "don't" list.

"I was born in Nikolayev. The town was named for the Tsar Nicholas II, you know?"

"Nana, today in school we had tryouts for *Oklahoma.*" Rache's mind was racing. "It's a musical, you know, and I tried out for the . . ."

But Nana Sashie cut her off.

"And it was on the Bug River . . . yes, it was the Bug River and . . ."

" 'Boog,' what a weird name. How do you spell it?"

"*B-U-G,* as in insect, but you say *Boog.*"

Rache tried again. "I auditioned for the part of Ado Annie —it's the second lead—"

"Yes, the Bug River. I don't know where it started, this Bug River . . . Poland maybe, or someplace in the Ukraine . . ." She paused.

"Well, anyhow it's the second female lead, not the first, but I think it's more my type of role."

"The Ukraine, probably."

"Livelier, not as mushy as . . ." Rache was a little desperate. Nana Sashie was talking about the old country, and both her mother and father said that this always upset her so much that she wouldn't eat for two days.

"On Papa's day off he would take me to the park. And I would always say, 'Please Papa, no Yiddish in the park, just Russian!' "

"Why would you say that, Nana?" Rache couldn't resist any longer.

"Well-l-l-l." She dragged out the word and cocked her head while raising her nonexistent eyebrows. "My dear, in those days it was quite dangerous to be a Jew in Russia."

"What do you mean 'dangerous'?" whispered Rache. Thoughts of Ado Annie had evaporated.

"You really want to know, do you?" Nana Sashie leaned forward a bit. Playing Rache like a fish, she wanted to be sure that the hook was set.

"Yes! Yes! I really do."

"Your mother and father will be upset—your making an old lady remember!" Her eyes had a hard glitter for a moment.

"Well, I don't care," said Rache stoutly. "I can't stand talking about school."

"And I can't stand hearing about it," said Nana Sashie in a very grouchy voice.

They didn't talk about school any more.

"THEY just liked to kill people, I guess." Nana Sashie pressed her lips together tightly and gave a little shudder. "We had nothing they could envy. We were not permitted to own land. But they would come and burn down Jewish villages. Your own great-great-great-grandma and -grandpa were murdered in their beds."

"Murdered!" Rache was stunned. The word took on a new horror. She could hardly believe that she was the great-great-great-granddaughter of "murdered" people. It was sickening. Weird. Grandparents weren't supposed to be murdered. They had heart attacks and died.

"Yes, murdered," continued Nana Sashie. "And the soldiers who did it stole two silver wine cups—the only things of value that they owned."

"Why did you stay there?"

"We didn't, silly girl. We left. Escaped!"

"You! You escaped?" Incredulous, Rache stared into the calm eye of the woolly storm that rocked back and forth in front of her, as if to seek out another body, another person beyond this one. "How did you do it? Tell me! Tell me!"

"It's a long, long story, more than can be told in one afternoon."

"Well, start now."

"Rache!" Her mother's voice shouted from the kitchen. "Time for your dentist appointment."

Rache slapped her forehead. "I can't believe it!" she muttered. "Just a minute!" she shouted back.

"You'd better go," said Nana Sashie, and patted her hand. "It'll keep, not too long, but it'll keep." Rache got up to leave, then stopped at the door.

"Nana . . ."

"Don't worry. I'm not going to die while you're at the dentist. Now go on."

❖ ❖ ❖ ❖ ❖ ❖ ❖ ❖ **III** ❖ ❖ ❖ ❖ ❖ ❖ ❖ ❖

NANA Sashie kept her word. She did not die while Rache was at the dentist. But between Rache and Nana Sashie's story was an interminable number of errands and unforeseen events. There was, to begin with, the dentist appointment, then a trip to the cleaner's, than a trip to Nana Rose's to pick her up and bring her back for dinner. When they arrived home, Nana Sashie was dozing. Then there was dinner, which went on forever, and then Nana Sashie went to sleep during dessert. So Rache's father carried her up to bed. Then there was homework. Then when Nana Sashie woke up later in the evening, Nana Rose and her mother descended upon her to teach her some "marvelous rhythmic breathing exercises" that Nana Rose had learned in her Golden Age Yoga Club.

"Why are you doing that to Nana Sashie?" Rache asked, watching from the doorway to the bedroom.

"We're not doing it *to* her, darling," Nana Rose answered. "It's *for* her, and she can do it all by herself in bed. Now inhale slowly, Mama, one-two-three, to the mid-chest level—hold it— It will help her," Nana Rose continued on the exhale, "make her more relaxed."

"She's so damn relaxed she's always sleeping as it is!"

"Rachel!"

"Rachel!"

"Rachel!"

All three generations exploded in unison. For a moment, standing in the doorway, Rache was caught by the striking similarity of the three women's faces. Just as they shouted her name, their faces, despite the obvious age differences, appeared to be almost identical—the eyes wide and lively with shock, the broad fore-

heads and brows knotted and creased, the high rounded cheek-bones becoming even more prominent as their mouths broke into the exclamation that was her name. It did not matter that Nana Sashie's hair was thin and white, Nana Rose's lacquered and steely gray, and her mother's short-cropped and prematurely salt-and-pepper. Did she, Rache, look like them, she wondered? And Nana Sashie's murdered great-great-grandmother, what did she look like?

"Really, Leah, you must do something about this child's mouth," seethed Nana Rose. Nana Sashie was a bubbling cauldron of Yiddish.

"Rachel, go to your room right now." Rachel began to protest and her mother whisked her into the hallway. In an exasperated hiss she began to talk. "I know 'damn' isn't the worst word in the world. I know you could have said a lot worse. But Rache, you know how the nanas are! I don't want two strokes on my hands!"

Later, Rache's father knocked softly on her bedroom door. "Who is it?" she asked, her voice thick with sulking.

"Me. Dad. Do I detect a third stroke about to occur?"

"Come in." She sighed.

Ed walked in and sat down on Rache's bed. "Look," he began, "I know it's tough sometimes, and I think the Senior Citizens' Yoga Club—"

"The Golden Age Yoga Club," Rache corrected.

"Well I think—"

"I don't want to talk about that," she said suddenly, turning to her father. "Is it true that my great-great-great-grandparents were murdered in their beds?" A tense energy burned through her sulking tone. Ed looked baffled. "Well yes," he said slowly, "but God, that was years ago. Is that what you're upset about . . . not Mom and Nana Rose?"

"Yes, of course," Rache nodded, trying to keep her voice from trembling. "Arguments with Mom and Nana Rose are daily events, but murder!"

"Well, unfortunately, murdering Jews was then almost a daily event in Russian history."

"What do you mean? How did it happen?"

"Just the way the Nazi holocaust happened. People—those in power, the so-called leaders—take a group of people who, because of their looks or practices or beliefs, appear slightly different from the majority. Anything different can be perceived as a threat. These leaders begin to think of the differences and not the things they have in common. Gradually they dehumanize these people, make them into abstractions. It's very easy to kill an abstraction. And your great-great-great-grandparents had become that to the Russian government."

"But why?" Rache's eyes were round with horror.

"Because it was convenient. The Russian tsar at that time, Nicholas II, was a weak-minded boob. He was probably a very nice guy socially. That's the thing that's creepy about all these types. But the country was wracked with problems—economic, social, whatever. Nicholas had a real classic bad guy for a chief adviser. I can't remember his name now. It began with a *P* or something. But this same guy had also been his tutor, I think. In any case, he was completely under the thumb of the bad guy, who started whispering things in his ear about Jews. After all, it had worked before—using Jews as targets. You know, set up

a scapegoat and the other people, the majority, will temporarily stop blaming the government and vent their anger on something else, some imaginary evil. It's been done time and time again in history."

"You just start saying these aren't people because they have long noses."

"Exactly, or dark hair, or they talk differently, or have yellow skin and slanted eyes. You stop thinking of them as moms or dads, or children or families."

"Or grandparents," added Rache.

"Yep. And then you can kill so easily."

"And that's what they did?"

"Yes. Quite systematically—mind you, not with the technical expertise of the Nazis. They didn't have gas chambers, death trains, and concentration camps. It was more of a hack-and-burn operation. They'd come through Jewish villages and just level them, killing everybody. 'Pogroms,' they were called."

"Phew!" Rache let out a long low whistle. The two of them sat quietly for some minutes without saying anything. Rache looked up at her dad. She had succeeded in making him look almost as disturbed as she felt. His brow crinkled in a way that was quite different from when he was working over an architectural problem at his drawing board.

"Gee, Rache," Ed said as he got up to leave, "I hope you won't ever talk to Nana Sashie about all this. To her it's all quite real, you know. It's not just history."

"You mean it's family!" Rache responded with a trace of defiance.

Ed colored. His face swam with confusion. "Well, yes, I guess so. Goodnight, Rache. Don't worry about this too much." He gave her hand two short pats and kissed her on the forehead.

The next day was worse.

"I'd like to resign," Rache said soberly to Miss Klintock, the drama teacher.

"Resign, dear? Resign from what?"

"From being curtain-puller."

"Oh!" Miss Klintock's bright-pink lips formed a perfect O as she said the word. It was the expression of a concerned but not too bright woman. Miss Klintock genuinely liked kids, and they liked her, even though she was in a constant state of bewilderment about young people and never to the slightest degree felt any need to try and understand them. That was for education majors, not drama coaches.

"It's not that I'm disappointed about not getting the Ado Annie role." Rache had wanted to set that straight right away. "It's just that I don't really have time now for the after-school rehearsals."

"Well, what would you have done if you had gotten the Ado Annie part?"

"I guess I would have had to resign."

"Well, now, this really does present a problem." Miss Klintock ran her fingers through the mop of orange frizz that seemed to float about her scalp rather than grow from it.

What could be such a big deal problem, Rache wondered. She absolutely hated this kind of situation. Why should she feel guilty for not wanting to be curtain-puller?

"Miss Klintock, my great-grandmother lives at home . . ."

"Yes, I know, dear. How is she?"

"Well . . ." Rache's voice trailed off, leaving Miss Klintock to fill in her own catalogue of horrors.

"Oh, dear . . . oh, dear!"

"Well," Rache said quickly, "and it's just that it's important that I be able to talk to her. She needs company now, and my mom's . . ."

"Oh, I understand, dear. Yes! Yes! Of course. But if only just today you could be curtain-puller, just today? Then I'm sure I can arrange things. Yes, we'll work something out."

"Sure! Sure! Today, no problem." Relief! She'd done it without lying. She hadn't really told the truth either. But listening to Nana Sashie was one hundred times more important than being curtain-puller for Klintock's production of *Oklahoma*.

❖ ❖ ❖ ❖ ❖ ❖ ❖ **IV** ❖ ❖ ❖ ❖ ❖ ❖ ❖

THE next afternoon Nana Sashie began. Rache sat right by her chair, and when Nana Sashie forgot where a sentence was going, Rache would repeat the previous sentence for her and together they would head off again in the true direction.

"I had overheard them—Mama and Papa talking in the kitchen of our small apartment. I was supposed to be asleep, but the apartment was only two rooms, so it was hard not to hear when something interesting was going on. And this was interesting. Papa was mad—very mad—about the tsar, about the army, about being a soldier. He had served four years in the tsar's army and had never been completely discharged. He could still be called up.

" 'It's an outrage! An absolute outrage,' he shouted, 'that we have to serve! One minute they burn Jewish villages. Then they call us up to defend their borders. I won't go, Ida! I won't go!'

" 'What can you do, Joe? What *can* you do?' my mother cried. I buried my head in the pillow and cried to myself.

"What would we do without Papa? It was unthinkable. I was already a girl of nine or ten, almost grown up, but I could not imagine life without him, Mama without him, or the babies— yes, there were two babies—without him. How old were the babies? Let me think a moment, Rache. Louie must have been about one and a half and Cecile five months. But most of all I couldn't imagine me without Papa."

Nana Sashie's faded eyes seemed caught in a flickering of dim memories. Stealthily, color began to seep into the ancient irises, a deep-brown flecked with twinkles and glints. Something seemed to be happening to Nana Sashie. There was still the old figure nestled in the layers of shawls and blankets. There was still the potato face. But it was as if the years were melting away. The eyes that had grown dim from seeing so much were now bright with anticipation, and her mouth parted slightly in the daring half smile of an adventurer. It was as if Nana Sashie were becoming Sashie, the little girl in the tintype on the mantel downstairs that Rache had seen all her life but had never really believed existed.

But Sashie did indeed exist. It was she, Sashie, with all her nine-year-old daring and crazy ideas, who came up with the escape plan for her family that Russian spring of 1900.

The family had decided to leave. "Enough is enough," as her father had said every night for the past year. But the decision to leave was nothing compared to actually doing it. It was not that simple for a Jewish family that included a young man of soldier age, his wife, two babies, one little girl, one grandfather, and a young old-maid aunt just to pack up and leave a country that was determined to keep you, either to kill you or to have you kill for it.

For a month after the decision was made there were heated arguments about the best way to escape. Of course, all these discussions took place at night. The adults would sit around the

samovar drinking tea and arguing in hushed voices after the
children were asleep in bed, for fear that they might spill the
beans to neighbors or that the neighbors might hear through
thin walls. Every grownup in the family had a plan of his own
and an insulting remark for every other plan. Zayde Sol's, the
grandfather's, plan was that they should do it after he died,
which he was sure would be imminently.

"Not that I wish you dead," said his only daughter, Ghisa.
"But why should I believe that you will die imminently—you've
never been on time for anything in your life!"

"The girl has a tongue! What a tongue!" muttered Sashie's

mother. She got up and gave a poke to the coals in the draft chimney of the samovar.

Ghisa had a plan too. Ghisa's plan was that the family let her work through her contacts at the Nikolayev artists and writers club; they could "arrange things" for them.

"Not those radicals! I will not associate with those dirty, moth-eaten, smelly radicals!" Sashie's father exploded. Sashie had no idea what a radical was. As she listened in bed to the word being batted back and forth in hoarse whispers, she thought it sounded like a dangerous flower or something from her father's toolbox—a special wrench or maybe even an exotic bolt. Sashie's father was a machinist at a factory outside Nikolayev. He always carried his own toolbox for the repairs on the machines he operated. He was very particular about the tools, but he let Sashie play with them, and she had already begun to show a certain skill and care in the way she used tools.

"Radical schmadical," snorted Sashie's mother. Ida had a knack for taking the mystery out of things. "They're a bunch of nincompoops who couldn't pull off their own shoes, let alone an escape. So keep your artists and writers to yourself, Ghisa."

Sashie was inclined to agree with her mother. Whenever Ghisa had brought home any friends from the club, their behavior had always seemed a bit peculiar. There was one fellow who, once he began speaking, became so passionate about whatever he was saying that he would forget about his cigarette until it burned his fingers. It made Sashie so anxious that she sometimes went down the hall to play with Moishe, a neighbor child she could barely tolerate. Another one of Ghisa's friends Sashie and her mother had named "Mismatch" because he never wore anything that matched. He would arrive with one black sock and one gray one. His pants would be too baggy and his jacket too tight, or one pantleg would be too short and the other too long. Even his beard seemed to grow more thickly on one side of his chin than on the other.

Any plans arranged by Ghisa's artist and writer friends, who had now become "contacts" in the dangerous and tricky business of escape, were bound to be botched. Sashie knew this as well as she knew that Moishe cheated at marbles. "Count me out," she muttered in the darkness, the same words she had said that afternoon to the miserable Moishe. But Sashie had no real intention of being counted out. In fact, she was working out the details of her own escape plan, learning from listening to the others and determining the strong and weak points of each one. Ghisa's plan was all weak points, obviously, but to Sashie's mind, her mother's plan had potential. The only problem was that it was not a plan. It was just a notion, which she always began with the same words: "I think we should just look like we're out for a Sunday stroll—very casual."

"You plan to stroll all the way to the border—casually?" Ghisa would retort each time. Unfortunately, Sashie's mother could never get any further than the "casually" part of her idea, and "casually" was not a word to inspire much confidence. Consequently, the idea would always fizzle on the spot. But for some reason it would never quite fizzle in Sashie's mind.

Her father's plan was even vaguer than her mother's. It was a machinist's view of the universe: oil a screw here, tighten a bolt there, find a loose nut, a little grease for the bearings, make sure no threads were stripped—the machine runs. In a rough translation: you find a friend here who knows somebody there who can (in payment for an old debt) arrange something with somebody who knows a corruptible border guard who, greased just right, opens things up and lets the little family slip across the border some moonless night. It was definitely a machinist's view of things, but in this case Sashie's father did not know the machine at all and would be as skillful in dealing with its innards as a watchmaker trying to repair a locomotive. Sashie's father was not the kind to have influential friends or connections or even contacts. So he did not know if any nuts could be turned or bearings oiled.

"Crazy," rasped Zayde Sol.

"Mr. Wheeler-dealer!" Ghisa's voice was tinged with mockery. "Just who do *you* know who will help us? Just what big mucky-mucks do you have indebted to you? The tsar, perhaps?"

"Joe," said his wife with gentle resignation, "for a machinist, for a man who works all day with lathes and drills and bolts and pins and . . . and"—Ida's hands grasped the air as if there were a wrench there—"and things that you can hold in your hands and feel their weight, you sure are a dreamer!"

Still, for Sashie the plan had appeal, and just as her mother's notion of a Sunday stroll out of Russia kept stirring in some cavern of her imagination, so did her father's notion of people "out there" who could help them. Night after night Sashie listened to them argue. Night after night she tried to figure out just what would turn notions into actions, ideas into facts, dreams into reality. There were people out there who could help. Of that Sashie was sure. They were not big mucky-mucks, as Ghisa had called them, but they were not Zev or Mismatch either. They might be decent people and they might be cheats. But they had one thing in common: they were all desperate, and because of this they would help.

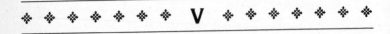

"HELP! We need help down here! The dishwasher's gone bananas and is overflowing! Rache, quick! Bring big bath towels, we're having a flood in the kitchen."

Rache smacked her forehead with her hand and remembered not to say "Damn." "There's not a moment's peace around here!" She seethed.

"Rache!"

"Coming!"

As Rache came down the back stairs into the kitchen she heard snatches of her mother and Nana Rose's conversation:

". . . always up there with Nana Sashie, Mom."

"So what's the harm?"

"I worry."

"Don't make worries for yourself, Leah."

"Maybe I should find out what's going on up there?"

Rache tensed and moved down a step in the hallway to hear better.

"Maybe you should find out what's going on with this dishwasher."

Hooray for Nana Rose, Rache cheered silently, and then clambered noisily down the rest of the stairs and came into the kitchen with an armload of towels.

"It's not a kink in the hose," said Rache's dad later that evening. He was underneath the sink with a flashlight, straining and sweating and twisting his body like a contortionist in order to look at the dishwasher's plumbing.

"I wish you wouldn't wear your nice pants to do this in," Leah said.

"Would you prefer I do it in the nude?" he gasped. Rache thought he looked just like a plaid pretzel doubled up under the sink.

"Ouch!" There was a fleshy thud of metal and scalp meeting. "There's going to be a kink in my brain from that one. . . . No, it's definitely not in the hose. It must be the drain tube's valve. And," he said with a groan, "it's a job for a troll or Nana Sashie."

"You're not stuffing Nana Sashie under there!" screamed Nana Rose.

"No, no . . . calm down, Mom," soothed Leah. "Ed will get it off so she can work on it right here."

Nana Sashie was sitting in her downstairs kitchen rocker, as she often did around dinner time when Leah was cooking.

"If it's corroded, I won't have a thing to do with it," Nana Sashie sniffed.

"If it's corroded, I won't be able to get it off, so don't worry."

In another minute Rache's father emerged from under the sink, sweat and a trickle of blood running down his forehead. In his hand he clutched the valve, which he handed to Nana Sashie with relief. She examined it closely for a full minute.

"Threads are probably gone," she offered matter-of-factly. "Get the toolbox, Rachel."

"No, no. It's too heavy for her. I'll get it," Leah said.

"No, it's not!" shouted Rache as she ran for the back hall closet. She had seen the box every day of her life, but it had always been just a dark wooden box, stained and nicked, its corners worn to a smooth roundness, its hinges blackened with age. The old latch that had fallen off years ago had never been replaced. There was nothing special about this box's appearance. It was so plain and so ordinary that one would hardly look at it twice. It blended in with all the stuff in the closet—the mops, the dustpans, the brooms, the rags, the aprons. Yet when Rache came back with it in her arms, she looked as if she were carrying the most precious thing in the world, or at least the long-lost silver wine cups of Nana Sashie's murdered grandparents.

"Put it here." Nana Sashie indicated the low table next to her chair. Murmuring something about a new latch, she flipped open the box's lid. As she did so, a tiny staircase of partitioned trays stepped out and the strange Cyrillic letters ИЯЛ appeared in dark relief inside the lid of the box. Nana Sashie's fingers, light and quick as hummingbird wings, ran over the initials, then darted for a sliver of a screwdriver in one of the compartments. She tried a turn. "Needs penetrating oil." The hands flew back to the box and in a lower compartment found a small can of oil, which she squirted around the head of the bolt. Rache, her parents, and Nana Rose stood silently watching Nana Sashie work. They seemed transfixed. It didn't bother Nana Sashie. She was used to audiences for these things.

The phone rang, splitting the silence.

"If it's for me, tell them to call back," said Ed, not shifting his gaze as Leah went to answer.

"It's for Rache."

"Who is it?" she asked not turning her head.

"It's Amy."

Rache made a face.

Her mother covered the phone with her hand. "I think she wants to make up," she whispered. "Why don't you talk to her?"

Rache made another face and waved her hand as if to say, "Hang up" or "Kiss off."

"Rache, come on! The least you can do is talk to her."

"Oh, all right!" Rache stomped over to the phone and took

the receiver. She turned so she could still see Nana Sashie, who was now working with a tiny awl and gouging out the head of the bolt so she could get a better purchase on it with a screwdriver.

"Hi," said Rache in a rather distracted voice. "Yeah," she said in response to something that Amy had said. "Yeah," she said again and then again, her attention never veering from Nana Sashie. In the two-minute conversation with Amy, Rache had said "yeah" and only "yeah" fifteen times.

"What was all that about?" her mother asked.

"I'm going to help Amy with the Ado Annie part. Her singing stinks."

Nana Sashie continued to work. She had completely taken apart the valve. She had been right. Most of the bolts were in bad shape. Indeed, some of them had been corroded, but with a little oil and a bolt extractor she deftly drew them out of their crusty lodges. Some of the smaller bolts were beyond repair, but the salvageable ones, once cleaned, were rethreaded in the ancient thread dies.

Nana Sashie's hands were old hands that often shook with tremors and ached with arthritis. She could not get rid of the ache, but she could control the tremors by bracing both her elbows against the arms of the chair. Her stiffened, gnarled left hand, which was useless for fine work, she used as a kind of vise or clamp. To others, even her own family, it seemed miraculous that Nana Sashie could do this kind of work, but as she said, "When you get arthritis at forty and plan to live past seventy-five, you figure out ways." Within the hour the valve was reinstalled and Nana Sashie had dozed off in her chair.

Except for the unfortunate presence of Brussels sprouts, dinner was cheerful. Nana Sashie continued to doze at the table for fifteen more minutes, thus avoiding the Brussels sprouts and waking up just in time for dessert.

"Have a lot of homework tonight, Rache?" her mother asked.

"No, but I promised Klintock that I would cut out three vests for the cowboys in the play."

"You!" exclaimed her father. "Sew a costume for a Klintock production?"

"I have to or else I'll get a C in drama for lack of interest. So I'd rather do something I can do at home. Besides, I don't have to sew them, just cut them out."

Rache's mother breathed a sigh of relief, as she most likely would have had to do the sewing.

"Is this for Purim?" asked Nana Sashie.

"*Oklahoma* for Purim!" giggled Leah.

"A real first, Jewish cowboys!" Ed said with delight. "Butch Cohen and the Sundance Kid!"

"What's *Oklahoma?*" asked Nana Sashie.

"It's the musical our class is giving."

"Well, when I hear 'costumes,' I think of Purim. That's what it always meant to me." She spoke in a way and with a look that had come to bear special meaning for Rache.

"I'll cut out the vests in your room, Nana Sashie, and keep you company," Rache offered quickly, and then excused herself to go upstairs to get her things.

As she left the room, she heard Leah say to Nana Rose, "See what I mean?"

Again Nana Sashie's almost translucent eyes seemed to turn brown in a flickering of dim reflections from unimaginable distances. Rache's scissors stopped cutting as she watched the mysterious transformation.

"Oh, do I remember that night!"

"What night?" asked Rache softly.

"The night I got it . . . the plan."

The night that it came to Sashie, the plan, what should be done, was a night when, oddly enough, there had been no arguments about the escape. Instead there had been a quarrel about Purim, the most festive and gayest holiday of the year. Purim celebrates the downfall of a tyrant and the joyous victory of the freedom-loving Jewish people. Sashie loved the Purim story. She delighted in the perfect justice, the neat twist at the end. Esther was the beautiful Jewish queen of King Ahasuerus, ruler of the Persians and Medes. Her cousin Mordecai refused to bow down before Haman, the king's counsel. Outraged, Haman plotted the slaughter of all the Jews in the kingdom. Hearing of the plot, Esther risked her own life in a confrontation with the king when she spoke out to save her people.

For Purim there were always costumes and music and sweet things to eat. There were plays and carnivals and games and dances. But that year none of the grownups seemed to have any enthusiasm for it. Sashie's mother had half-heartedly promised to make hamantaschen, the triangular poppy seed cookies that were supposed to look like the villainous Haman's hat. Every time Sashie had asked Ghisa about making Purim costumes, however, she was put off. The last time she had asked, Ghisa had burst out angrily, "Costumes! How can you think of costumes at a time like this!"

"Now, Ghisa, go easy on her," Sashie's mother had warned. "She's just a little girl."

"You baby her," Zayde Sol had countered.

"Stay out of it, Pop," her father had said sourly.

Tempers had been short for days, but Sashie had never seen her father speak to his father in this way. She went off to bed that night feeling awful. How could she think of costumes and cookies at such a time? What was she, some sort of imbecile? Some thick-headed unfeeling kid? Or just a "little girl"? She felt guilty and sad and angry all at once. Then just when her cheeks were hot with tears and she had a feeling of disgust burning deep in her stomach, the idea came to her. It stilled her body and made all the dark feelings of anger and shame evaporate like so many raindrops in sunlight. Lying in the darkness quietly thinking, Sashie rested her eyes on the samovar. Its polished brass caught the glow of the gas lamp outside. It helped her concentrate to watch it, burnished and radiant in the winter night. She felt she could almost see her brain at work, see the silvery glints and flashes as ideas connected, and she had the eerie feeling of being a witness to her mind. She stepped so quietly out of bed that no one heard her, and when she appeared in her thin white nightgown in front of the grownups, they all stopped what they were doing, for she looked so odd and wraithlike.

"The child's unwell!" Zayde Sol whispered.

"You want to throw up?" Her mother started toward her.

"No! No!" Sashie raised her hand to stop her, then looked

around at the family. She could feel the heat of the samovar through her thin gown. "I know how we can escape."

Their eyes wide, the grownups listened to Sashie with a concentration usually reserved only for other grownups. "We must go on the eleventh day of Adar," Sashie declared softly, "and we must go as Purim players."

There was a deep silence. Then the silence began to crackle, not with the usual insults and mockery that greeted the other escape plans, but with the excitement and energy of quickened heartbeats and pulses, with the joyous short breaths of people about to be free!

❖ ❖ ❖ ❖ ❖ ❖ ❖ ❖ **VI** ❖ ❖ ❖ ❖ ❖ ❖ ❖ ❖

GHISA'S eyebrows collided to form a dark knot over the bridge of her nose and her spectacles slid down a bit. "There's a problem." Ghisa raised her hand as if to quell Sashie's fear. "Not to say it can't be solved!" This was Ghisa at her most gracious. Even Ida blinked at her sister-in-law's new charm. *"But—"* She dropped the word with all the subtlety of a pig plopping in mud, then paused, relishing the suspense in which the family hung. The old Ghisa again . . .

"But schmut! Get to the point, Ghisa," Ida shot back.

"But"—Sashie shivered now in her nightgown—"it's a three-day trip to the border, right?" Not waiting for an answer, Ghisa went on in a rapid hiss. "Purim is the fourteenth day of Adar.

We must leave a full three days in advance. We tell people we are going to a nearby village—to Melivka or Karinovka, right? —to celebrate with family. Well, now, tell me this: what are we going to look like leaving on the eleventh day of Adar, three whole days before Purim, all gussied up on our way to a village just down the road. People won't believe it." A clammy silence fell on the family. Darn Ghisa! Sashie thought. But she was right. The family would look odd dressed up and leaving so early for a celebration supposedly just down the road. Five minutes earlier the air in the small room had crackled with joy. Sashie marveled at how fast things could change.

Ghisa sensed the change in the room too. "It's a problem— that's all." Her voice had a trace of apology.

Her father having moved slightly beside her, Sashie looked up. His body had become taut with a new kind of energy. His fingers twitched slightly. "It's a problem, Ghisa, yes," he said crisply, cutting off his sentences so they would not explode senselessly. "That is right. You are also right that problems have their solutions!" It was the machinist talking. His eyes were bright, boring into Ghisa. "That is precisely the difference between problems and tragedies. There are no solutions to tragedies. They can't be fixed, but we"—his voice rose with exuberance—"we have a problem, but the overall plan is workable. Now the problem," he said, lifting one finger in a professorial manner, "is how to appear to be going for a Purim celebration down the road, when we are actually traveling to the border, without arousing suspicion. Logically it seems impossible." As soon as Sashie heard her father say "seems impossible" she knew he had an answer.

"I've got it!" Ghisa exclaimed. "We must leave Nikolayev under cover." She spoke the last word with such an air of lofty authority that one might have thought she had been a consultant on all the major escapes in Eastern Europe. It irritated Sashie a bit, but she preferred Ghisa in this mood than in the other. "And"—it was Ghisa's turn to raise her finger—"not in our Purim costumes. They must wait until we are within a day of the border."

"An excellent idea!" said Joe. Why was her father letting Ghisa have the credit? Sashie was bewildered. It was apparent that he had known the answer too. But the mood was lively and full of promise again, so Sashie did not waste time pondering such inscrutable behavior.

"But!" The pig plopped again.

"Ye gods!" Ida rolled her eyes toward the ceiling and sighed. Her exclamation sounded like air going out of a balloon.

"There are no 'buts,' " Joe retorted. "Just state the problem, Ghisa."

"How then do we get out of Nikolayev? Do we steal away in the night, costumes tucked under our arms? An old man, two babies, a child . . . ?" Ghisa's eyes widened in disbelief. "I mean, a family of seven loaded with belongings is hardly unnoticeable. It's . . . it's like . . . well, a chicken you can hide, but an elephant people notice." Ghisa at the time didn't know how prophetic her remark was.

"What's this about elephants?" Zayde Sol's face danced with a bright confusion. "We're going on elephants?"

"Glad you both mentioned elephants!" Joe piped up. Was he joking or what, Sashie wondered. She had never seen her father in such a mood. "We must travel light," he continued. "There will be no belongings taken, no extras."

Ghisa and Ida appeared shocked at this pronouncement. "What do you think this is?" Joe leaned forward to make his point. "In this escaping business, you don't take the candlesticks, the pots and pans and slop pails. You take your bodies, and that's all. The idea is to get across the border, not set up housekeeping on it!"

Sashie looked at her father in amazement. He's really going to solve the problems, she thought to herself. He'll make it happen! He's fantastic! Joe's positive approach was contagious.

"Ghisa!" Ida interjected suddenly, "when you make the costumes, make them reversible, with one side plain. Then we won't have to carry them. We'll just wear them inside out for the first day."

"Exactly, Ida!" Joe exclaimed.

Even Ghisa was impressed with this idea. "Nice plan. It will take a lot of work, very careful cutting, but I can do it."

"Of course you can!" Joe patted her shoulder.

Still, something bothered Sashie about the plan. The first two days of the journey seemed vague, not quite specific enough. Something was incomplete in the cover part of the undercover, or was it the under part of the cover? But she couldn't quite put her finger on the fault. Then suddenly she spoke. "We need a horse and wagon."

"A horse and wagon!" Ghisa almost shouted, then began to chuckle to herself as if she were enjoying some private joke. "Well, my dear, you might as well have asked for an elephant." Even Joe seemed incredulous. For a family that had never

stoking the furnaces. Occasionally he ventured upstairs into shipping or toolmaking, but he always chose a route that tunneled through the highest stacks of crates or past the machines that had the fewest people working them.

When new employees came to work at the factory, they learned when the breaks were, where to relieve themselves, and to avoid Wolf. There was no need to inform them explicitly of the last; it was immediately apparent. Those who were curious enough about Wolf might make inquiries among other workers. There would then be vague references to Vishnagova and Vesnatefka, Jewish villages in the north that had been obliterated by the tsar, where streets had turned black with blood and where there were no survivors. But once the names of the villages were spoken, people rarely asked any more about Wolf. One time a young shipping clerk had fainted straight away when she rounded a corner and nearly collided with Wolf in the maze of stacked boxes. Later, after she came to, she whispered repeatedly to a girlfriend, "It's his eyes—the eyes . . . the eyes." She was thinking about those pupils, frozen like pinpricks of terror in the pale yellowish irises.

Joe thought about all this the next morning as he stood at his the turning a bearing shell. He thought of Vishnagova and Vesnatefka as he cut metallic curls from the steel disks. Other people needed full concentration while working the lathe; for the tool was almost an extension of his arm, the spinning ion as soothing and mindless as top spinning is for a child. Upon arriving at the factory at six that morning, he had gone directly to his lathe rather than any of the other machines he with. He needed time to think. So now he thought—

of Vishnagova and Vesnatefka; he thought of the villages' dreadful epitaph, "No survivors, not even a cat," and then the inexplicable arrival of Wolf and the swirl of chilling rumors. Joe had been a sweep-up boy of nine or ten when Wolf had first come to the factory. Now he was a senior machinist. He put another bearing shell on the lathe and began cutting. Things change, he mused, but Wolf doesn't. The haunted face, the eyes like beads of terror—it was as if this man had been fossilized at some cataclysmic moment in the earth's history: a dinosaur trapped in quicksand as the cutting edge of the ice age racked over the plains, a springing jack rabbit entombed in molten lava, their eyes transfixed forever by the vision of the horror that was about to engulf them. Joe had read about such events in books. There was only one difference: the events in the books were part of the earth's natural history. Vishnagova and Vesnatefka were part of man's history. This made them almost unspeakable in their horror, unimaginable in their inhumanity. He thought about Wolf—the eyes, the eyes. Joe knew what the girl meant. Wolf was no survivor. He was the living dead.

"He's not the desperate one," thought Joe. "I am. He's dead. . . . In this case, he's got the advantage." The irony stunned Joe as he stood there, swaying in the heat of the furnace room, trying to bring into focus the figure that dissolved in the shadows. It was a ghastly place, this furnace room! Joe's head swam in the intense heat. Manic shadows cast from the hot, glowing furnace grates pranced like demons. Oh, to be back at the lathe! Joe thought. It had taken him all day to work up his courage to come down here. The work day had finished half an hour before.

Joe had waited as long as possible before coming down. He knew Wolf would still be there, stoking up the furnace to keep the heat at maintenance level for the night. Never mind about cold workers, but cold machinery turned out inferior parts. Joe's eyes were burning with tears from the heat. He squinted to sharpen the focus, but everything appeared wavy and quivering through the screen of heat and tears.

"Wolf!" There was no answer. He leaned forward and peered into the shadows. "Wolf!" A low sound came from the darkness; it was hoarse, a kind of painful growl. "I . . . I . . ." Joe stammered, "I want to talk to you." There was more silence, a deep dark well of silence. Joe refused to fall in it. He clapped his hands together and rubbed them in an absurdly casual gesture considering the churning he was feeling inside. "Well now," Joe's voice became almost conversational, "you stay down here most of the time?" He looked around then and, not waiting for an answer, he continued. "Pretty hot. No need for heavy clothes even on the coldest days," Joe prattled on. "One might even say this is tropical compared to upstairs!" He clapped his hands together as if to applaud this witty choice of the word "tropical." "You must leave off your sweaters as soon as you arrive in the morning."

First there were some gasping noises as if air were being forced through old pipes after a long while, then the croaking voice said, "I live here."

Joe's jaw went slack. The hands preparing for another jolly clap dropped to his side.

"You live here?"

"Yes."

Joe felt real panic. I must get out of here, he thought. Why in the name of God am I consorting with this *meshuggener* creature in this hellhole . . . ? It's not decent. . . . I'm a husband and father. . . . I live . . . Then Joe thought of that little pinch-faced girl and her dingy wisdom. Damn her, he thought, it's not supposed to work this way, Sashie. I'm not supposed to be the desperate one. He is.

"We are both desperate people." Joe heard himself speaking the words as if he were standing outside his own body. "You and me, Wolf, we're both desperate." At that moment Wolf stepped out of the shadows.

"You want help."

Joe was not sure whether it was a question or a statement. He could now see the figure clearly before him. Despite a large frame, the man appeared shrunken and hunched. Wolf's face, although deeply lined, had a strange waxy smoothness. His beard was ill-grown and patchy, and his eyes . . . his eyes! Joe began speaking rather than looking at those eyes.

"My family . . . we . . ." There was a pause. "We have decided to leave." Joe whispered the words so softly that he was not sure Wolf had heard them. "We must leave"—Joe stopped again, then looking straight into the haunted eyes—"in order to survive as a family." The pale-yellow eyes flinched as Joe spoke the last words. Perhaps it had been cruel of him to use the words with such calculation, but it was the truth and it was his trump card with Wolf.

Wolf cocked his head, jutting his chin out defiantly. The face was a twisted horror. "You think I know about families?" The hiss of self-hatred cut the air.

Joe felt his knees begin to buckle. He put out his hand to grab something and it met with Wolf's shoulder. It was just enough to steady him. Then, as if to cover up the reason for his hand being there, Joe patted Wolf's shoulder lightly, as an older man might pat a small child.

"Look," Joe said, taking a deep breath, "there is no need to talk about that. I have a wife, a father, a sister, and three little ones. We want to leave on the eleventh day of Adar." Joe repeated the date in Yiddish. "I need a wagon. I need a contact at the border." He paused again. "We need your help. I can offer you some money, but not much."

This deal, this plea, was so far beyond the ordinary that it was needless, in fact silly, for Joe to even speak of payment. The words "not much" seemed to hang in the air, not as a goad to

more payment, but as a reflection of Wolf's very existence. Wolf stared unabashedly at Joe as if to say, You idiot! I am nothing. Why offer anything at all?

Joe was overcome with embarrassment. "Well . . . well . . ." he began to stammer. Then cutting short his words, he solidly placed his hands on Wolf's shoulders and, giving them both a friendly shake, smiled and said gently, "Prettier faces I have seen!"

Wolf looked stunned, but then, like the first great watery bubble pushing its way upward through an artesian well, there was a deep shake of laughter and then another and another.

"See you tomorrow," said Joe with a nervous chuckle, and turned and left.

That evening at home Joe passed up his customary glass of tea that had been brewing all day in the samovar and went straight for the cabinet where he kept a small bottle. He poured himself a tiny amount of the clear liquid and shot a glance over the rim of the glass that said, "don't ask" to his family. He told them nothing that night of his meeting with Wolf Levinson.

❖ ❖ ❖ ❖ ❖ ❖   **VIII**   ❖ ❖ ❖ ❖ ❖ ❖

H E doesn't look half bad, thought Joe the following day as Wolf stepped out from the coal bin, shovel in hand. This time as soon as Joe had seen the last worker put on his coat, he had made his way to the furnace room. He had heard the scuttling and scraping sounds in the coal bin. For a fleeting moment his stomach tightened and his throat locked, but then he managed to call his name, and as soon as Wolf stepped out, Joe felt better. Wolf barely looked up, but went about his business carrying a shovelful of coal to a half-opened grate of one of the furnaces. He kicked it open the rest of the way, heaved in the coal, and shut it. Wolf walked around to the furnace's other side and opened wide two large drafts. The huge furnace sucked in great gulps of air like a dragon starved for oxygen. Within seconds there was a deafening roar of fiery combustion that seemed to shake the whole building. What in the name of God is he doing, Joe wondered. Joe moved closer to him to talk over the roar, but Wolf was not finished. Carefully he propped the shovel and walked over to a wall where a broom hung. Wolf motioned for Joe to pick up a dustpan that was near him and to come. He then began to sweep, keeping his head down. Joe bent over, holding the dustpan while trying to keep his ear cocked directly below Wolf's mouth. Wolf began to speak in a low rasping voice that blended perfectly with the hisses and sizzles, those smaller fiery sounds beneath the roar of the furnace.

"I must deliver a wagonload of chickens," Wolf said, emphasizing "wagon," "for the boss. The chickens travel first class. You go second."

"What do you mean?" asked Joe, hardly able to contain his excitement.

"I mean you go underneath the chicken coops. There's a space about sixteen inches. You lie flat. But it's not far."

"How far?"

"Just to Stepinova."

"Stepinova!" He jerked up from the dustpan only to hit his head on Wolf's broom and feel himself shoved down by an iron hand.

"Shut up!" Wolf spat. "Listen to the rest. I get you a wagon at Stepinova for the rest of the trip to the border—no chickens. At the border there's a sentry. More about that later. But one thing: sentries don't take paper money. They take only gold."

This was indeed a problem. Leaving Nikolayev under cover had been easily if not comfortably solved, but now they had to hide gold too. How would they hide it all? After they had sold their belongings for the money—however meager a sum—to have to convert this into gold would still be awkward. It would be so heavy considering how lightly they wanted to travel, and so noisy. Paper bills could be stuffed anywhere, but gold? The dozens of gold pieces they would need! Where? How could they? It was too much of a problem to think about. Joe sat down on the floor in a state of complete distraction. Wolf touched him lightly on the shoulder. "I'll meet you in the alley behind the cobbler's row at two in the morning on the eleventh day of Adar."

"Gold! It isn't the gold!" That's what Ida said when she heard about it. "It's the chickens! We gotta go with *chickens?*" she hissed in a whisper.

"Well, it's only for a little way, Ida. Then another wagon—no chickens."

"How far, Joe?"

"Just a short distance."

"How far, Joe?"

"Well," his voice grew smaller, "Stepinova?"

"Stepinova!" And everybody knew exactly the picture Ida had in mind. Ida, the immaculate housekeeper, the mother of pink, chubby, scrubbed babies, stretched out with her three children under the clucking blizzard of chicken feathers and droppings.

Zayde Sol was not overly disturbed by the prospects of traveling with chickens, as he felt sure that he would be dead by the departure date. Ghisa, although not enthusiastic, was for the first time in her life pleased that she wore spectacles. Joe had grown accustomed to the idea. And Sashie was ecstatic.

GROSS!, Rache thought as she sprawled across the light-blue shag rug in Amy's bedroom. This is absolutely the grossest thing I've ever seen. In front of her, Amy, gesticulating like an automated mannequin in a window display, was singing Ado Annie's "show-stopper" song, "I Cain't Say No."

Amy now launched into the main refrain, her braces flashing as she opened her mouth wide.

"I'm just a girl who cain't say no."

When she sang the word "no," Amy's longish freckled face became even longer as she pulled out the "no" into a ridiculously elaborate sound.

"I'm in a turrible fix."

Rache winced on "turrible." Oh, God, she thought, she's trying to sound western, and it sounds like baby talk with a New York accent! Amy had moved from New York just two years before and had not lost any of her accent.

"I always say, 'Come on, let's go.' "

On the word "go," Amy turned and beckoned over her shoulder in a gesture that was identical to the traffic lady's at the corner of Elm and Walsh when she motioned the kids to cross.

Total grossness. There was no other word for it. Rache's father said "gross" was the most overworked word in the adolescent lexicon. He was constantly after Rache to use more "descriptive" words, a "richer variety," but he hadn't heard Amy yet. Rache lay there, a weak smile fixed on her face, eyes glazed, trying not to betray her feelings.

"When a person tries to kiss a girl,"

Amy panted and bobbed her head in a display of—what? Rache wondered, What in the world is this supposed to be? Amy's idea of sexy?

"I know she oughta give his face a smack!"

On the word "smack," Amy smacked her own cheek. For crying out loud, Rache thought.

"But as soon as someone kisses me I somehow sorta wanna kiss him back!"

The panting and bobbing again. Rache thought fleetingly of the composers. Rodgers and Hammerstein would be so grossed out at this.

"I'm just a fool when lights are low."

Amy rolled her eyes and smirked. This must be her idea of seductive, Rache guessed.

"I cain't be prissy and quaint."

She curled her hands up into little paws and drew them to her chest chipmunk style, her elbows tucked close to her sides, and pranced around on her tiptoes.

"I ain't the type that can faint."

I might vomit though, Rache thought.

"How can I be what I ain't?"

She's the daughter of a New York physicist and she grew up one block from the Metropolitan Museum. She went to Columbia University nursery school and before she moved here she'd never been west of New Jersey!

"I cain't say no!"

The tape recorder clicked off. Amy's face resumed its normal contours as the "no" expired on her lips.

"Well, what do you think?"

Rache was silent, stalling for time, stalling for a word. "Well . . ." she began.

Amy's chin moved slightly. Her large lower lip pushed out. "Pretty gross, huh?"

Rache looked at her tall, gangly friend—freckles aquiver, eyes cast down. "No," she said quickly. "It's fixable."

"I can't do it!" Amy wailed, and collapsed like an ailing giraffe on the rug. "You know why they gave me this part?" she whined. "They think I need a 'confidence builder.'"

"Klintock isn't that perceptive," Rache countered.

"It wasn't Klintock. It was the guidance counselor—Tompkins."

"Tompkins!"

"Yeah."

"How do you know that, Amy? Come on."

"I know," Amy said with authority. "I know." Then abruptly she changed the subject. "What have you been doing lately anyhow? You're never around. And you would have forgotten to come if I hadn't called you this afternoon."

"No, I wouldn't have."

"Yes, you would. You're always busy."

"Not really."

"Who've you been hanging out with?" Amy asked warily.

Rache looked carefully at her friend. Why not say it, she thought; she could trust Amy, of all people. "My great-grandmother," she replied simply.

"Come on!"

"It's the truth. But you can't tell anybody."

"What?" Amy looked puzzled.

Rache pushed the *Oklahoma* score aside. "Amy, I'm talking to Nana Sashie about things I'm not supposed to be talking with her about. And it's absolutely fantastic."

"What do you mean? What kind of things?"

"It's about her life. Before she came here—well, really, how she came here . . . from Russia."

"Well, why can't you talk about it?"

"My parents think it's bad for her, makes her sad."

"What's sad about it?"

"Nothing. It's fantastic! Do you know that when she was just nine years old, she planned—I mean plotted, almost by herself —the family's escape from Russia."

"You're kidding!" Amy's eyes opened wide. For the next half-hour Rache told Amy what Nana Sashie had told her.

"Well, then what happened?" demanded Amy.

"I don't know. My mother called and said that we had to go get Nana Rose and take her to the osteopath."

"You mean, they're actually going to get in that wagon with those chickens?" Rache nodded silently. "Oh, how gross!" Amy exclaimed. "You know, Rache, you should put this down. Write a story about it. It's really—" she paused, and thought—"it's so much more important than this." She kicked the music for her song off the rug.

"Look, we've changed the subject long enough, Amy."

"No we haven't." She stopped. Her face knotted into a fierce scowl. "Has it ever struck you that our lives are exceedingly boring? I mean, really, Rache, these productions, the clubs, the cheerleading, cafeteria rules, proms, Senior Day, honors math, dumbo English—who thinks up all this crap?"

"Come on, Amy!"

"What do you mean, 'come on'!" Amy was off and running. "Guidance counseling! What a joke! Tompkins has just left his second wife. He sees his kids alternate weekends and he's being paid to guide us! Him and his damn confidence-building schemes. He's a total mess. I build his confidence. I'm one of the few undivorced people he knows."

"*Look!*" Rache shouted to break through, "you got this part and it's too late to back out now." She picked up the music and handed it to Amy. "You're just going to have to show them that you can do it," she said firmly, although she wasn't sure how this was going to be accomplished.

"How?" Amy echoed Rache's thoughts. "Ado Annie is supposed to be little and cute and 'pert.' " She spoke the last word as if she were tasting a loathsome medicine. "It's just not me . . . it's Cheryl Beech."

"That's it!" said Rache with sudden inspiration. "It's not you!"

"I just said that."

"You've got to quit playing it as if you wished you were somebody else."

"I don't get it."

"You gotta cut out this cutesy-pooh stuff. And you must, you absolutely must drop that phony hick accent—it's just gross! And furthermore, stop all this business . . ." Rache did a quick medley of the gestures Amy used to punctuate the song. "You look like a cross between a flamingo and a basketball player."

"Thanks a bunch."

"Well, it's really weird looking."

"Well, what am I supposed to do up there?"

"Nothing. Just play it straight with your New York accent and your hands stuck in your pockets. Pretend like you're trying to solve a calculus problem." (Amy was the only ninth grader taking calculus.)

She looked skeptical.

"Try it," Rache ordered and got up and put on the recorder. Amy started into the song's introduction.

"It's not so much a question of not knowing what to do . . ."

"Put your hands in your pockets!" Rache barked, as Amy began to gesture.

"I've known what's right and wrong since I was ten . . ."

She was stiff, but there was a new earnestness, a new reality.

* * * * * * * *   X   * * * * * * * *

"I KNEW it was right immediately!" Nana Sashie snapped her fingers in the air loudly. It was such an uncharacteristic gesture for an old lady, but that's what Rache loved—the transformations, the odd juxtapositions, the slidings back and forth between two realities: the young gestures with the old memories, the mysterious new light in the ancient irises, the adventurer disguised in shawls.

"What was right?" Rache asked suddenly. She had become so mesmerized by the transformation that she had forgotten to ask what Nana Sashie was talking about, and Nana Sashie had the habit of beginning right in the middle of a thought.

"The hamantaschen, of course."

"Of course," said Rache. She was treading lightly. "Uh, Nana?"

"Yes?" Nana Sashie cocked her head very sweetly and looked at Rache inquiringly.

"What about the hamantaschen?"

"I thought you'd never ask!"

Sometimes Nana Sashie could be quite exasperating.

"Well, I'm asking. What was the big deal with the haman-taschen? A cookie's a cookie. Right?"

"Wrong. Not these." Nana Sashie paused.

"Nana Sashie, I don't mean to rush you, but it's just half an hour until my piano lesson, and . . ."

"You know I really don't know why they insist on piano lessons. You're not that musical. You don't seem to have inherited the Bloom musical talent. I think carpentry would take you a lot further."

Would she ever get Nana Sashie back on the track?

"But I guess it's none of my business."

"Right!" exclaimed Rache.

"Wrong! You were wrong about the cookies. They were not ordinary cookies at all."

"What was special?" Rache pressed.

Nana Sashie leaned forward out of the mohair blizzard and whispered in a low voice, "they had gold!"

Rache caught her breath, then began tentatively, "You mean . . . the gold problem?" She drew her face close to Nana Sashie's. She wanted to get this straight. "That's how you solved it?" Nana Sashie nodded smugly. Her mouth and eyes compressed into three little slits as she relived the utter cleverness of it all.

"Ingenious—my mother!"

"Your mother thought it up?"

"My mother!" Two small tears squeezed out of the slits.

"The gold is no problem," Ida announced two days later after the evening meal. Sashie, Joe, Zayde Sol, and Ghisa looked at Ida expectantly. They were still sitting at the table. Ida was cuddling baby Cecile in her lap. She moved closer to the table and lowered her voice to a barely audible whisper. Her round dimpled face beamed with a conspirator's delight. "Sashie!" Her brown eyes twinkled as she looked at her daughter. "Your wish will come true!" Sashie looked perplexed. "We'll make hamantaschen tomorrow night and into each cookie we'll fold a piece of gold!"

"Ida!" gasped Joe. "You are a genius!" Joe jumped up and ran around the table and lifted his little round wife, still holding their fat little baby, right up into the air and danced them both around the table. The baby squealed, Sashie giggled, Joe sang, Ghisa chuckled, Zayde Sol tapped his foot, and Ida smiled and said in a sing-song voice, "I still can't stand the chickens, Joe!"

By the next day operations were fully underway. Ida had been to the market, an excited Sashie dancing at her side, and bought large supplies of flour and sugar for the cookie dough, and dried fruits and poppy seeds for the filling, for Sashie, in a rare moment of caution, had suggested that two batches of hamantaschen should be baked—one with the traditional fruit filling and the other with the gold. The gold hamantaschen would be buried under the real hamantaschen and would give the family something to nibble on. Joe was in charge of getting the gold. By exchanging paper money and selling most of their possessions, which were not many, they could just cover the bribe. A lovely silver necklace made by an uncle of Ida's had to be sold. Joe commiserated over this more than Ida.

"You looked so lovely in it!"

"So maybe there'll be another one someday. You never can tell."

Ghisa rummaged through her remnant bag and came up with enough fabric that, if cut and pieced just right, would work for costumes. With some money she had saved, she bought a few shinies, as she called them—gold braid and bright tassels to embellish the costume side of the reversible outfits she was making.

"Let's not have a Haman, Ghisa," Sashie said, turning from the bowl in which she was mixing the flour, sugar, eggs, butter, and baking powder for the dough.

Ida looked up from the simmering pot of dried fruit she was stirring on the stove.

"I agree. There are enough Hamans out there. We don't need one in the wagon with us."

"Well," said Ghisa, "it's up to you, but everybody has to look like a player—which player is his own business." She paused. "I suppose you want to be Queen Esther, Ida?"

"I have no preference, my dear girl," she said with a groan as she lifted the pot of stewed fruit off the hot part of the stove. The pungent scent of cinnamon and apricots swirled through the air. "If you would like to be Queen Esther, you're welcome to it."

"No, really," said Ghisa as she carefully sandwiched a panel of heavy cotton batting between a piece of dark wool and a piece of quilted crimson fabric, "I think I might be . . ." The words came slowly through a row of pins clenched in her teeth, "Queen . . ." She stopped, removed a pin from between her teeth and stuck it into the crimson quilting and the batting. "Vashti! Yes, Queen Vashti!"

"Queen Vashti!" said Sashie, incredulous.

"Vashti!" chuckled Joe.

"Nobody's ever gone as Vashti," said Sashie.

"Now, how do you know that, Sashie?" Ida asked, suppressing her laughter.

"But, Mama!"

"But Mama!" mimicked Ghisa, then changed to a more serious tone. "I think she was a smart lady. She needs more recognition." Vashti was King Ahasuerus's first wife. She had been banished because she had refused the king's demand. "How would you feel," Ghisa continued, "if your husband ordered you to appear dressed only in your crown, so he could prove that you were the most beautiful woman in the land?"

Sashie giggled.

"I'll tell you what I'd tell him!" said Ida. "I'd tell him to go jump in the slop bucket!"

This did it. Sashie doubled up in a fit of giggles on the floor. Joe put down the Yiddish newspaper he was reading and, looking at his wife, tried to imagine her dressed in just a crown and him in a slop bucket. He began to laugh at the idea. Soon he was laughing so hard that he woke up Zayde Sol.

"What's so funny? What's so funny?" Zayde Sol kept asking for a full two minutes, but everyone was laughing so hard they couldn't answer him. "Maybe I'm dead," he muttered to himself, "and they can't hear me. It's not so bad." Then he began giggling too.

The laughter finally subsided. Joe pulled on the samovar

handle to draw himself more water for his tea. He stifled an errant chuckle or two and began to speak. "You know, I hope Ghisa, that you weren't planning on me for the King. I'm beginning to have doubts about this fellow." He put a sugar cube in the back of his mouth to suck on while he drank the tea.

"Well," Ghisa said, "if Ida's Queen Esther, it did seem fitting that you be King Ahasuerus—but as you like. These Purim spiels aren't an exact science, you know."

"I think I'd prefer to go as Mordecai."

"Fine!" said Ghisa, turning to Zayde Sol, and saying, "You're King, Papa!"

"Of course," Sol nodded.

"What am I going as?" demanded Sashie.

"You can be Hatach," answered Ghisa.

"Who's Hatach?"

"Who's Hatach?" Ghisa opened her eyes wide in mock amazement.

"Well, who is she?" persisted Sashie.

"*He* was the king's servant who ran messages between the king, Queen Esther, and her cousin Mordecai."

"I have to be a boy? I'd rather be a girl."

"Well, for you, we'll make Hatach a girl then," Ghisa said cheerfully. "As I mentioned before, it's not an exact science, these plays."

"What kind of messages did Hatach send?" Sashie asked warily.

"Well, it was through Hatach that Esther learned of Haman's plot to kill the Jews."

"And all because Mordecai wouldn't bow down to the wicked Haman," Sashie filled in. She loved this part of the story, and of course the part where Esther speaks out, risking her own life, and tells the king to stop Haman's plot to destroy her people.

"Mordecai was a pain in the neck," Ghisa said with a laugh. "But Haman would have found another reason to wipe out the Jews even if Mordecai had bowed down."

"We should all have a pain in the neck like Mordecai," Ida added.

"And then what happens?" Sashie urged. She knew what happened next, but adored hearing the story.

"And then . . ." Ghisa paused while placing the last pin. "And then the king finds out that Mordecai was involved once in saving his life and the king says, 'What can we do to honor a hero?' And Haman thinks the king is talking about him, not Mordecai, and says . . ."

" 'Dress him up fancy!' " Sashie exclaimed.

"You depart from the text, dearie." Ghisa looked over her spectacles and intoned, " *'Let a royal garment be brought.'* That is the way it is written in the SCROLL OF ESTHER."

" 'Bring him a royal horse,' " Sashie continued.

" *'Bring a horse on which a king has ridden and on whose head a royal crown has been placed,'* " quoted Ghisa.

"And then?" asked Sashie.

"And then everything happens: the king hangs Haman because Esther told the king what he had plotted. Mordecai is made an adviser to the king and, most important, takes the king's message to Jews in every city. He tells them that they are not to be destroyed, but to gather together and protect their lives, and instructs them to forever after keep the fourteenth and fifteenth days of Adar, for these are the special days on which the Jews were saved, days of sorrow turned into days of gladness, days of mourning turned into days of holiday. No more tyrants!"

"Huh!" muttered Ida under her breath.

Suddenly Sashie felt uncomfortable. The turn-the-tables perfection of the story, the neatness of the mix-up, and the even trade of bad for good, sorrow for happiness, that she had always delighted in unnerved her now. It was too perfect.

"Come on, Sash. Time for the fun part. Joe, get the gold," Ida said. "Bring it over here where I've rolled out the dough."

She turned to Sashie. "Now, we'll have to experiment a bit. I think Haman's hat will have to be bigger this year. So let's make the circles about this size." Ida indicated a four-inch diameter with her fingers.

"All of them should be that way." Sashie added, "You shouldn't be able to tell the difference between the gold-filled and the fruit-filled ones."

"Good idea! Also, I think we'd better put some fruit filling in the gold ones too, just to fill out the pouches so they won't collapse when we're baking them."

Sashie and Ida began the job. Each circle was filled with a teaspoon of the fruit mixture and a gold piece, then two of the sides were drawn up and the third folded across, so that a triangle was formed, the same shape as Haman's hat. The seams were pinched together, and finally each cookie was brushed with beaten eggs to turn them golden brown. Fill-fold-pinch-paint, cookie after cookie.

"Ah, you do yours so neatly, Sashie. Perfect!"

Sashie felt a queasiness in the back of her throat as her mother said the word "perfect." She deliberately began to make some of the hamantaschen look less than perfect—a messily pinched edge here and there, still tight enough to conceal the gold, but not perfect.

By 2:30 the next morning, Ida and Sashie had completed the baking. Hundreds of triangles, pouched, plump, and golden, lay cooling on the cookie sheets, ready to be packed.

"WELL, it doesn't have to be so perfect, Mom."

"But it should be wearable, and these . . ." Leah held up some faded cheesecloth fragments that looked as if they had served half the moth population of the city. "This is all the costume department could come up with?" There was a mixture of disgust and amazement in her voice.

"Yep. That's why I asked you to help sew. Amy needs all the help she can get."

"So you said. What did they use these *schmattes* for anyway?" Sometimes only a Yiddish word would suffice.

"The Christmas pageant," Rache replied.

Leah's face assumed a perplexed look as if to say, Oh, these Christians and their inscrutable ways!

"I think they were shepherds' costumes," Rache offered.

"I think the actors might have really herded sheep in them," Leah muttered. "Anyhow, they're beyond hope." She tossed them back into the bag. "Now, what was it Klintock said? 'Something cute and Western, sort of square-dancey'?"

"Forget the cute part. We're trying for something a little more . . . more, well, sort of—uh—Barbra Streisand-ish."

Now Leah really looked perplexed. "Ye Gods." She rolled her eyes toward the ceiling. "Listen, go down to the basement. You know where the remnant boxes are?" Rache nodded. "Okay. I think the box on the left has a couple of yards of decent gingham."

"Gingham? That doesn't sound like Barbra Streisand to me."

Rache's dad walked through the living room eating a corned beef sandwich.

"Don't complicate the issue, Ed."

"Well, it sounds more like Debbie Reynolds. You gotta get this corned beef sliced thinner, Leah."

"Who's Debbie Reynolds?" asked Rache.

"Who's Debbie Reynolds!" Ed almost screamed in shock. "Who's Debbie Reynolds? Gad!" He slapped his forehead in mock horror. "Leah, did you hear that?"

"Well, who is she?" asked Rache.

"Look, kiddo, is this one of your amusing little tricks to make me feel like the Cro-Magnon man?"

"Look, I'm asking a simple question. Who's Debbie Reynolds —did she wear gingham or something?"

"Did she wear gingham or something?" Ed mused aloud. "Yes, quite a bit of it—spiritually if not actually." Then he turned to Rache and addressed her. "She's a movie star, very popular, but I guess before your time."

"Cute?"

"Yes, if you like that type."

"Go get the gingham," ordered Leah. "I guarantee Amy Schwartz will not look like Debbie Reynolds, even in gingham."

Rache went down to the basement. There were actually four remnant boxes. Her mother must have forgotten that she had brought two over from Nana Rose's, so it would take some rummaging to dig up the gingham.

"Who's Debbie Reynolds?" Rache giggled softly as she thought of her father's incredulous face. She loved these discussions with her dad. He gave her no credit for knowing anything prior to the Beatles—"the beginning of Western culture for you and your friends," he often said. The jibing was a good-natured game between them, "designed to close the generation gap." She laughed to herself as she thought how genuinely shocked her dad would be if he knew how far back into this century she was actually exploring. "If I said "tsar" to him, he'd probably think I was referring to a new rock group." Just then, deep in the remnant box her hand struck something cold and hard. She pulled it out. What in the world? The words formed silently on her lips. The object was made from some kind of metal, but it had obviously darkened with age. It was about seven or eight inches tall, with elaborate curves. There were some small slots in the sides, and the inside was hollow. The object did not seem complete in itself but looked as though it were part of something else, but what? A vase of some sort? Rache's fingers traced lightly over the surface. "This is something! Something from *then*," she said softly to herself. Her eyes flickered in an odd way, and when she said "then" she felt the pull backwards through time towards another reality.

"Rache!" Leah's voice came from the top of the cellar stairs. "What's taking so long? Where's the gingham?"

"Darn!" Rache fumed. "Never a moment's peace around here." She found the gingham and ran upstairs, the metal object in one hand and the fabric in the other.

Nana Rose had just arrived by taxi and was taking off her coat and boots.

"Hi, Nana."

"Hello, Rache. What do you have there?" she asked, looking at the object in Rache's left hand.

"I don't know. Do you?" Rache held out the object toward Nana Rose, who took it from her.

"Well, for goodness sakes. This is . . . this is . . ." she stammered. "Well, I'm not exactly sure. I haven't seen it for years. I remember something . . . Just where did you find this, Rache?"

"In a remnant box."

"Oh, the one I sent over to your mom?"

"Yes."

By this time Leah was examining it. "What do you call these things, Mother? Oh, what is it, you know . . ." Leah asked vaguely while scratching her head.

Rache was beside herself with impatience as the two women traded the object back and forth, turning it over in their hands. She knew whatever this was, it was terribly important. Yet the air was thick with the two women's vagueness and the stumbles and starts of their memory. Rache was ready to gag on the delays and the half-articulated thoughts. What is it? she almost screamed. Then suddenly Rache had a strange intuition. "Is it something for tea?"

"Why, yes, yes! I think so, darling. It's a . . ." Again there was an agonizing pause. "Oh, it's on the tip of my tongue . . . you know, Leah, one of those contraptions for making tea."

"You mean a samovar?" Rache asked in amazement.

"Yes!" the two women chorused. "Now how did you know that?" asked Leah.

Rache couldn't believe it. She stared at the object with its curves and little slots. A Russian samovar in their own house in Minnesota.

"How did you know that, Rache?" asked Nana Rose, her voice absolutely creaking with curiosity.

Rache thought fast. "Oh, we were studying stuff in school about Russia," she said quickly. "How did we get this one?" Rache asked.

"Well, from the old country, but I don't think it's a whole samovar," offered Leah.

"No, definitely not. Part of it is missing." Nana Rose was trying to muster some authority into her voice, which Rache was quick to pick up.

"Well, what part is it?" she pressed. "How did it work?"

"Well, I think something went underneath," Nana Rose said.

Something! Rache thought with disgust but tried to camouflage her exasperation. These two women are driving me crazy with their "somethings" and "on-the-tip-of-my-tongues." In their hands they held an object that had come eight thousand miles with their family from Nikolayev to Minnesota, and they had forgotten its name, its function, and how it worked. Rache knew more about it than they did. In all of Nana Sashie's stories there were references to the samovar and the tea, drunk through the evenings, that had brewed all day atop it. The samovar itself had never seemed of central importance to Nana Sashie's story, but allusions to it ran through her narration like burnished filaments, highlighting things here, connecting there. ". . . And then my mother turned the spigot of the samovar and added just a bit of water to Papa's tea because he liked it strong." Or ". . . Even the babies liked a glass of tea from the samovar." Or ". . . From my bed I could see the samovar standing on the table like a polished soldier, its brass catching the glow of the

gas lamp in the street outside. I used to pretend it was a good soldier, a sentry standing watch over us in the darkness."

Rache looked across at her mother and Nana Rose. The two heads, one completely gray, the other prematurely salt-and-pepper, were bent over the samovar part. They were murmuring vague words of curiosity, soft exclamations, and there were fragile references to "those days," "Old World," "the people." It was as if they were in a museum talking about artifacts in a glass case. Rache suddenly panicked. Supposing she were an old old lady and these women were her daughter and granddaughter. Was it going to be like this? She would be one of "the people" from "those days," the "Old World," those "dead days." They would probably think of her world as quaint. Rache hated the word. People always used that word to describe unreal storybook places that had no relevance to their lives.

"I don't know how the darn thing worked," Nana Rose said, "but don't ask her, Rache." She looked directly at her granddaughter as she issued the warning. "It's bound to upset her."

"Take it back to the basement so it won't get lost," said Leah. Her mother's remark struck Rache as exceedingly ironic, but she dutifully took it downstairs.

There was no decision to be made. As she went down to the basement, Rache knew that she would ignore the warning, retrieve the samovar part, and take it to Nana Sashie.

❖ ❖ ❖ ❖ ❖ ❖ ❖ **XII**❖ ❖ ❖ ❖ ❖ ❖ ❖

A STROKE! They'd absolutely have a stroke, thought Rache as she crept past her parents' bedroom. The house had been asleep for a good three hours. Rache had set her alarm and put it under her pillow. When the muffled buzz went off at 2:00 A.M., she quickly pressed the button and slipped out of bed. Padding through the night shadows, she blessed the wall-to-wall carpeting upstairs. Downstairs she navigated from rug to rug like one of those exotic swamp birds that walks on lily pads. She dared not step on the wide old floor boards and unleash their

cacophony of squeaks and groans. When she reached the basement door she descended only two steps, for that afternoon she
had, with clever forethought, tucked the samovar piece behind
a laundry bin on the landing so she would not have to risk the
entire creaky basement staircase.

As she retraced her steps, clutching tightly to the samovar
piece, she thought about the best way to wake Nana Sashie
without shocking her to death. Then she was at the bedroom
door. Luckily it was always left slightly ajar, so Rache did not
have to turn any crickety doorknobs. She merely pushed the
door gently and walked through. The room was pitch black—
darker than the rest of the house. Through the darkness she
heard the light, rhythmic breathing of Nana Sashie. It was odd
how the breathing did not sound particularly old; it could just
as easily have been that of a young child. It had an ageless
quality in the darkness and reminded Rache of ocean waves
lapping the beach with their infinite rhythms. It took a moment
for her eyes to adjust. She could make out the shape of the
empty rocker standing beside the bed. The room seemed more
gray than black now. The covers rose in a range of humps and
lumps that appeared like the dark profile of a rugged mountain
range. It seemed strange that Nana Sashie's slight form could
make such a range, but then Rache remembered the nighttime
set of shawls and scarves in which the old old lady wrapped
herself for sleep. She walked over to the bed. Her eyes were
completely accustomed to the darkness now, and Nana Sashie's
plump, smooth cheek was like a moonstone in the nightroom.
She slept with her hand at her throat as if she were protecting

herself. It looked odd, but Rache realized this was the way Nana Sashie always slept—the hand at her throat. "Nana Sashie," Rache said and touched the cheek.

"Rache!" The eyes flicked open.

"Nana!"

"What's happening?"

"Nothing." Rache was collecting her wits. "I'm just here."

"I know. What are you doing here at this hour?"

"I wanted to talk to you."

"Oooh, good!" Nana Sashie wiggled with relish. There was a slight movement down the range of lumps and humps.

"We've got to be really quiet. I don't think we should even turn on the light."

Nana Sashie nodded like an obedient child. It struck Rache that Nana Sashie seemed to be amazingly alert. She sensed there would be no digressions, no petulant meanderings. Perhaps this was Nana Sashie's hour, and maybe Rache should always come to her at two in the morning. Rache spent several minutes propping up Nana Sashie against numerous pillows.

"Nana Sashie," she began cautiously, "do you know what this is?" Rache's hands were trembling as she held the samovar piece. What if she caused Nana Sashie to have a heart attack? Gently she placed the piece in her great-grandmother's hands, and then, as if for safekeeping of not just the samovar but of everything, she enfolded the old old hands in her own. "You know it?" she asked.

"Of course, it's the top of the samovar. Where did you find it?"

For the next three hours until the dawn light pierced the nightroom, Rache sat on the edge of the bed listening to Nana Sashie, her hands wrapped around the old ones that held the samovar part. And this was the story of the samovar:

"We must travel light," Joe kept repeating, but Ida's and Ghisa's notion of light was considerably heavier than Joe's.

"We can't starve. We must have food with us."

"Wolf is arranging for food. He'll have it tucked in the wagon —and there's always eggs!" added Joe. Ida scowled.

"Look," said Joe, "we know there are a lot of things we must take—the hamantaschen, the toolbox . . ."

"The toolbox!" interrupted Ghisa. "Why the toolbox?"

Ida knew better than to even pose the question. Stifling his

anger, Joe drew a deep breath and began a laboriously patient explanation. "My dear sister, we should no more consider leaving without the toolbox than . . . than—Oh, how can you be so stupid!" he exploded.

"Now, now, Joe," calmed Ida.

"What if the wagon breaks? What if a harness gives up the ghost, what if . . ." Joe was swamping Ghisa in "what-ifs" until Ida broke through.

"What if there's work outside Russia for a genius with his hands!" The rancor fled Joe's eyes and he looked at his wife with relief.

"Okay, Joe, you made your point," Ida continued crisply.

"You made it," Joe corrected softly.

"Now," Ida spoke, "how about if we are each allowed something to take with us on the trip—something from our old way of life for our new one, just one thing, Joe?"

"All right. One thing, but there must be limits. It cannot be too big."

"How big?" Ghisa and Sashie both asked excitedly.

"Well, let me think," said Joe, scratching his head. "It should be able to be carried on your body and not in your hands, because we will need everybody's hands ready to help with the babies and to carry the hamantaschen. I would think . . ." Joe's eyes had a twinkle "that it should be no larger than a chicken."

"A full-grown roaster!" added Ida quickly.

"Okay, Ida. What is it?" Joe asked warily. "By what name goes this full-grown roaster of yours?"

Ida hesitated a moment, then in a small voice said, "Samovar?"

"The samovar! Ida, you must be kidding. It's the size of three full-grown roasters standing on top of one another."

"Ridiculous," hissed Ghisa, "that you should consider even owning one, let alone escaping with it!"

"The samovar is part of our life," pleaded Ida.

"It is a stupid, indulgent, bourgeois frippery!" scolded Ghisa.

"It's just plain big," sighed Joe. But Sashie was still stuck on Ghisa's description. What in the world was an "indulgent, bourgeois frippery"? In spite of the nasty tone in Ghisa's voice, Sashie loved the sound of this string of words. It reminded her of an enormous bouquet of carnations, or maybe a sticky kind of candy with sesame seeds. If she ever had a pet, Sashie decided, she would name it Bourgeois Frippery. The argument went on and on.

"Bourgeois shmorgeois, you've indulged in a glass or two of tea yourself from the samovar, my friend." But arguments were the flintstones of Ida's genius. Just as one thought a dispute was destined to go on in unending circles, an idea would ignite in Ida's mind. Her eyes would glitter madly. Sashie thought she actually looked quite witchy on these occasions.

"I've got it! I am Queen Esther, right?"

"Right," said Ghisa cautiously. "But surely that doesn't mean . . ."

"I need a crown, right?"

"Well, I suppose."

"Well! Who ever heard of a queen without a crown? In the bottom we'll pack the hamantaschen."

All eyes in the room riveted on the top part of the samovar —the double-tiered top piece with the gentle arabesque curves.

The small mushroom-headed bolts and decoratively pierced vents could pass for a crown.

Then Ghisa asked with a calculated casualness, "You, uh, plan to wear your crown the entire trip?"

"In a sense," said Ida cryptically.

"What do you mean?" asked Joe. "You know, Ghisa has a point. If we're going to all this trouble with reversible costumes, plain side out for almost two days, what's the use if you're trotting around wearing a crown on top of your head?"

"Who said anything about wearing it on top of my head?" There was a long pause, and as soon as Ida was convinced that everyone looked sufficiently bewildered and confused she continued, "Ghisa has her glasses. Joe and Grandfather Sol have beards." The others were really looking perplexed now. "But Sashie, the babies, and I, we have nothing!" Her voice mounted in intensity. "We must face this situation, these monster chickens, bare-faced!"

Immediately it became clear what Ida planned to do with the samovar. She would unbolt the two tiers that formed the top piece and use them as face shields for the "bare-faced"—a new minority. The babies would probably tolerate it only when they were sleeping, but at least it would prevent chicken droppings from falling into their open mouths. There was even talk—by Ida—of using the draft chimney for drinks of fresh air by guiding it up between the chicken coops.

Ida's idea for the multitudinous functions of the samovar was so bizarre, so brazenly overwrought, so elaborately crazy—it trod such a fine line between the practical and the impractical—that even Ghisa began to suspect it showed the telltale signs of genius. Joe was loath to criticize the idea for Ida had so intricately tied it to her chief horror—the chickens—and he had felt it would be a miracle if he ever got her into the wagon in the first place. Sashie had no real thoughts on whether she would actually use the face shield or the air tube herself, but in the back of her mind there was something very comforting about the idea of the polished good soldier that she had known for so long accompanying them on the trip, even if he was disassembled. The rest of her mind was busy trying to figure out what she would take on the journey that was no bigger than a chicken —or a full-grown roaster. She went to bed thinking about the things she owned.

There were not many. Sashie had a ball. She had a beautiful rocking horse that her father had made her. She had half a dollhouse that he was building for her, but now she supposed it would never be finished. She had a necklace of coral beads, the kind found in the ocean, which had always reminded Sashie of things faraway and adventurous. She would often put part of the strand in her mouth and taste the salt of unknown oceans. She took the necklace from the bedpost where it hung and gave it a quick lick as she lay in bed. It seemed quite unexotic now —ordinary pebbles that she might have found in the courtyard. She peeked out over the covers. The grownups had all gone to bed too. This was their last full night in the apartment, the only place Sashie had ever lived. All that had ever had any meaning for her was contained within these walls. The day after tomorrow she would wake up in the middle of the night and leave this place. The samovar stood in luminous authority, a sentry in the darkness. Was it reflecting the gaslight glow, or was it radiant in itself, Sashie wondered, distracted momentarily. It seemed to have an illuminating power of its own. But the coals were stashed far up in the interior chimney. It would be impossible to see their glow. The strand of coral beads was making her drool. Tomorrow morning, Ghisa had said, she would sew them into Sashie's costume. Sashie was indifferent. What could you do with coral beads besides admire them?

She thought about the other things she would prefer to take. She had a doll, Tovah, a dear old thing—smaller than a full-grown roaster too—soft with a stuffed head. She could easily pin it to the inside of her coat, and when they got to wherever their final destination was, maybe she, Sashie, would be all grown up and Cecile would be just the right age for Tovah. She had Tovah's wagon, of which she was very proud, for she had built it almost all by herself. Her father had done the sawing and drilling, but Sashie had designed it, done all the gluing, the pegging together, and the sanding of the pieces. It was not that big, but there was no way she could comfortably carry a wooden wagon on her.

Her thoughts went back to Tovah's softness, and she remembered something else, the beautiful counting book that Ghisa had sewn for her. Each page was a quilted patchwork scene using sheared and ribbed velvets and slippery satins and silks. It was more like painting with fabric than sewing. Page after page showed glimpses of Nikolayev, and carefully stitched across the bottom of each page was the word for the number in Yiddish, Hebrew, and Russian. The first page showed a single small street, the baker's alley that was near their house. There was one horse and wagon, one street lamp, one child running down the beautiful quilted street that Ghisa had made by cutting minute pieces of brown, tan, and black velvets and sewing them into a mosaic of cobblestones. On the next page there were two boys standing outside the *cheder,* the Jewish school, with two rabbis. Two dogs chased a boy riding a bike, on the back of which were two geese in a cage. The last page of the book, number ten, was a dazzling culmination of city life. Ghisa had sewn a picture of the park, Sashie's favorite place, selecting the most colorful bits of fabric to illustrate all the vendors with their carts, the balloon man, the carousel, the organ-grinder—here with ten monkeys dancing on ten leashes. At the bottom of the page there was a caption, but this time it was different. Instead of stitching words for the numbers, Ghisa had sewn the words, PLEASE PAPA, NO YIDDISH, JUST RUSSIAN in all three languages.

It still made Sashie furious when she thought of Ghisa's sour little joke. But she had known better than to show her anger when Ghisa gave her the book. It was indeed a bittersweet gift and she always felt mocked when she turned to the last page. But even with the joke and even though she had long ago learned how to count, the book had an irresistible charm for Sashie, and as excited as she was about leaving Nikolayev, there was a funny unexplained part of her that did not want to forget it completely. She reached down beside the bed, her hand groping in the darkness. She felt the smooth sides of the tiny wooden wagon, the sides that had taken her ten days to sand. She remembered how proud her parents were of her patience and diligence when after supper each night she would go to her father's tool chest for a piece of sandpaper and work for an hour or more finishing the wood. She remembered her own sense of accomplishment as the crude, rough wood became smooth and light and clean under her sanding hands. She had developed different strokes for different parts of the wagon. Sometimes she moved the sandpaper in a circular pattern, sometimes in a flurry of short back-and-forth movements. She had used quick whispery flicks of the sandpaper to make the pegs fit perfectly. In the process she had worn thin over ten different pieces of the paper.

Now her hand ran over the simple little wagon in the darkness, recalling the various strokes for each of the wagon's parts. It suddenly occurred to Sashie that after tomorrow nothing would ever be the same again. Her hand touched the soft face of Tovah, the head nearly bald and worn to a silky smoothness from nine years of hard loving. What should she take? She wasn't sure. Tovah or the book? These were childish things, she knew. But they were all she had. Should she not take anything? That seemed unthinkable.

❖ ❖ ❖ ❖ ❖ ❖ ❖ **XIII** ❖ ❖ ❖ ❖ ❖ ❖ ❖

MUCH to his profound amazement, Grandfather Sol woke up alive shortly after midnight on the eleventh day of Adar. And much to Sashie's profound amazement, she had slept soundly

until shortly after midnight despite her protests that she should not be made to go to bed because she was too excited to sleep. From her bed, in the earliest minutes of that new day, she watched the giant sliding shadows of her mother and father and Ghisa as they moved about in silent preparations. Her body felt tight and tingly with excitement. Everything seemed different at this hour of this night—the air she breathed, the light, the shadows, the creaks of the floor. Even her parents and Ghisa seemed to have a new authority, a new defiant grace. They were no longer the cozy, predicatable little Jewish ghetto family con-demned to apartment 23 of 64 Kreshchatik Street.

Ghisa came over at the foot of Sashie's bed and lay out the costume. Sashie sat up and Ghisa put a finger to her mouth to signal her not to speak. Ghisa had arranged the pile of clothes for quiet and efficient dressing. Underwear and new long, thick stockings were on top. Sashie pulled these on while still under the covers. There was a sweater that fitted close to her body. Over this she wore a flannel blouse with slightly ballooned sleeves that closed tightly at the wrists. Next came a flannel underdress, and over all of this an exquisitely tailored wool jumper that hung from the shoulders with a slight flair. On one side it was, in Ghisa's words, "brown as a mouse and plain as a toad," but the other side was quilted in a vertical rainbow pattern of dusty pinks and browns and oranges. The shoulders and neck were trimmed in decorative embroidered strips that could only be bought in a gentile dry-goods store. "Some ser-vant," Joe had commented when he first saw the costume.

"Wait till she puts on the apron and the babushka on her head," Ghisa had advised. The apron was actually the flannel underdress, which was to be worn outside when the costume was reversed. The babushka was the same plain brown color as the wool side of the jumper. Both the apron and the babushka toned the costume down a bit, but as Sashie put on the layers of clothing, the costume side in, she felt scandalously colorful and as brazenly decorated as a peacock. That it was all a secret, a camouflage, made it infinitely more delicious. She could almost feel each embroidered curlicue pressing into her flesh.

Finally she was dressed. Her mother motioned Sashie to the other side of the room where a light bundle of bedclothes was tied up. Ida and Ghisa helped tie it onto Sashie's back with a large shawl. They tied it intricately so that there were two large ends left in front. Ida brought over the sleeping infant Cecile and slipped her into the sling cradle that was made with the shawl ends. Ghisa and Ida now secured the ends in such a way that the shawl carried most of the baby's weight. The baby was so light anyway that Sashie thought she could carry her all the way to the border. A small samovar part had been tied on a ribbon and pinned to Cecile's bunting as a pacifier. Louie had been deposited into a wool-lined knapsack made by Ghisa and strapped to Joe's back. Joe's tool chest rested on the floor beside his feet. Ghisa carried a heavier bundle of bedclothes but nothing in her hands, which were free to guide her father, Zayde Sol. Ida's bundle was the heaviest of all. Wrapped amongst the blankets and sheets were the various samovar parts and, contrary to Joe's orders, some small loaves of bread and a he'll-thank-me-for-it-later brisket of beef. On one arm she cradled the large samovar bowl with the gold hamantaschen.

All was ready. Joe nodded toward the door and they walked

out of the room. Sashie looked back once at the toy wagon. It was *there* now, she thought, a wooden thing, one of many things they were leaving behind. She was *here* moving in a line between Ghisa and her mother with Cecile tied to her.

They stepped outside the apartment building into the night, the air thick with a spring fog. Buildings dissolved, streets had no ends, corners no angles. Gaslight was swallowed up into the white throat of the fog. Scarves of mist swirled around them. In their heavy clothing, the grownups appeared puffy and unsubstantial. It was a world without edges, without perimeters or reference points, a swirling white void, yet Sashie felt as if she were about to slip over the rim of something and begin a terrifying fall into nothingness. She began to feel prickly in the layers of flannel and wool. In the night air her face became slick with sweat and mist. A queasy sweetness hovered deep in her throat, and she felt as if she might gag any second. Her father was directly in front of her now. She wanted to hold his hand, but his left hand held the toolbox and with his right one he felt along the side of the apartment building, for the fog had become so thick that Joe had to navigate by touch in order to find the corner of the building so he would know where to turn off of Kreshchatik Street onto a smaller one that led to the cobbler's alley. Incredibly the fog grew even thicker, and Sashie could barely make out her father's back with Louie in the knapsack. She reached out her hand towards the toolbox to keep her fingers lightly on the edge. She could not feel it, but behind her Ida's hand touched the bundle tied to Sashie's back, and behind Ida, Ghisa had Sol's arm linked in her own. The fingers of Ghisa's other hand found the mushroom-headed bolt of a samo-

var part that had worked its way through a hole in Ida's bundle. Linked together in a fragile chain of blind touch, the little family turned the corner and dissolved into the mist.

XIV

"RA-CHELLE! *Ma petite jolie cochon, venez!*"

Rache's dad's French accent was about as terrible as Amy's country-hick one, but he adored the sound of French and anyone speaking French, even himself. He called her "his darling little pig," not because she was fat—Rache was hardly that—but just because he loved the sound of the word *"cochon."* Utterances in French usually signaled that Ed was cooking or about to begin to. Rache enjoyed cooking with her dad immensely. It was an inexact science, which he made even more so. As she walked into the kitchen Rache noticed a light dusting of flour over the counter and floor.

"Must you always call me *'cochon'?*"

"Oh, I love the snuffy little vowel sound of it all!" He was in an ebullient mood to say the least.

"Well how about *'poupon'?* It has a snuffy little vowel sound."

"Ah, splendid! *Ma petite jolie cochon poupon!*"

"Wonderful," muttered Rache. "Now I'm your darling little pig doll."

"Come on help me with this cake for your mother's birthday."

"How many are you baking anyway, one for each year?" Rache surveyed what seemed to be a multitude of various-sized cake and cupcake pans.

"Ha ha, very funny. Your mother would love you for that one. No, for your information I am not. This seeming infinity of cake pans"—Ed gestured with a floured hand to the array—"will unite in one monumental structure to celebrate your mother's birthday."

"What, may I ask, is the monumental structure to be?"

"*Le Tour Eiffel.*"

"The Eiffel Tower. Are you crazy? That's going to be impossible. It'll break. It'll fall over. Why the Eiffel Tower?"

"Because we did not go there on our honeymoon," answered Ed matter-of-factly.

Rache was utterly perplexed. "Was it that bad?"

"What?"

This was beginning to remind her of conversations with Nana Sashie. "Your honeymoon," she said with exasperation.

"Oh, no, we had a wonderful honeymoon. It's just that we went to Banff and Lake Louise and, uh, you must admit that although it's a wonderful place for a honeymoon, it doesn't make it in cake terms. I mean, all you could do is two bowls of green jello edged with whipped cream."

"Gross."

"Rache!" Ed scowled as she said the word.

"Okay, okay, bizarre!" She paused. "Well, if you've ruled out Banff and Lake Louise as a cake, there are still a lot of other places that would be easier to make. Why not the Taj Mahal? It would be a lot more stable and you could bake the dome in that small mixing bowl."

"The Taj Mahal happens to be a mausoleum built for an emperor's favorite wife. Now, I think that would be bizarre for your mother's birthday. One might even say 'gross'! No, the Eiffel Tower is an elegant structure perfectly suited to your mother."

"Well, you know what you should do, if you want the Eiffel Tower? You should bake it all in one pan and then cut it into little pieces and stack them. It would be easier."

"I'm glad you're not an architect." Ed was one. "I'm baking these individually so that they will be structurally sound units. Then we will really be able to stack them. Do it your way and all you'll get is a lot of crumbs. Come on now, help me put the pans on these cookie sheets and get 'em in the oven."

While the cakes were baking, Rache turned to the pleasant task of licking the beaters and bowl of left-over batter. Ed began chopping onions for a vegetable dish.

"Dad, what's your favorite building in the whole world?"

"The Parthenon," Ed answered without hesitation.

"The Parthenon?"

"Rachel, for God's sakes, you have heard of the Parthenon, haven't you?" Ed turned from chopping the onions. There were tears streaming down his face. He took off his glasses to wipe his eyes with a dish towel.

"I know, I know," Rache said to reassure him. "It's the one in Greece."

"The one in Greece!" Ed muttered, and rolled his teary eyes

toward the ceiling. "Yes, that's the one, Rachel! And contrary to current adolescent opinion, Western architecture did not begin with the golden arches of McDonald's. There were a few precedents."

"Did you know that they're copyrighted?" Rache asked excitedly.

"What?"

"The golden arches."

"No, I did not." Although he was wearing Leah's strawberry-print apron and had flour on his nose, Ed suddenly looked dreadfully serious. He walked over to the counter where Rache was sitting and placed a hand on top of hers. "Rache, does that really impress you—that some guy got his design for these golden arches copyrighted and made a bundle? I mean, is that what you consider achievement? Quality?"

Rachel squirmed and looked down. "Dad, you know that I love the city pocket park you did and the library—even though you went into the hole on it. You know I think they are better."

"I know they're better! I don't need you to tell me! But I get concerned over your . . . your . . ." he stammered. He didn't want to use the word "values." It seemed too strong. "Your sense of . . . well . . . gads, you seem so impressed!"

"Dad, why don't you worry about things that other parents worry about, like grades, staying out late, or getting pregnant?"

"*Getting pregnant!*" shrieked Ed. "Are you trying to give me a heart attack!"

"No. But most parents worry about stuff like that."

"Look, you can make straight A's, and come in every Saturday night by eight o'clock, and never get pregnant until you've been

married five years and have a three-bedroom house, but if you
think that the greatest thing going in terms of human achievement is some guy who got his design for a hamburger stand
copyrighted, I am going to be concerned!"

"I don't think that at all, but you've got to admit it's interesting—the copyright part."

"I admit it. But so is the Parthenon!"

The cakes had cooled and Rache and Ed were now assem-
bling the Eiffel Tower, using the thick vanilla icing to hold the
ever-diminishing cakes one atop another. As soon as the pieces
were stacked, Ed began work with a pastry bag, squirting a

decorative latticework of chocolate that was supposed to suggest the steel beams of the tower.

Leah had been kept out of the kitchen for most of the day, and the dining-room doors had been closed after Rache had set the table. In the living room before dinner, Ed served martinis to Leah, Nana Rose, and himself. Nana Sashie drank a glass of kosher wine, which was watered down because of her borderline diabetes, and Rache had a Coke with a maraschino cherry in it.

"You know," said Rache as she swirled the cherry by its stem in her glass, "what I'm having is much worse for me than what you guys are having."

"Oh, really?" said Leah. "Why is that, dear?"

"Well, you know how they banned red dye #2 because it causes cancer?"

"Yes," said Leah, her eyes riveted on the glaringly red cherry.

"Well, they didn't ban it for cherries because if they did the whole maraschino cherry industry would collapse."

"Quick! Get that girl a martini!" said Ed.

"Well, that's scandalous!" huffed Nana Rose. "Rache, go over and wash off that cherry immediately." Rache rolled her eyes in disbelief.

"I'm not going to buy any more—that's awful. What's with this government, always protecting big business? It's disgusting. There must be a way you can make cherries without using a carcinogen," said Leah.

"Beet juice," offered Rache.

"Beet juice!" exclaimed Ed. "Who wants a beet-juice cherry lurking in a Coke? That ranks with apples and raisins for Halloween. People who do that should be locked up."

"Open your presents, Leah!" said Nana Sashie.

"Good idea," Rache said, and reached for a basket of gaily wrapped presents. "Open this first! This first! Please! It's from Nana Rose and me. You'll never guess what it is. Read the limerick first and then try and guess."

"I take no responsibility for the limerick." Nana Rose raised her hand in a disclaiming gesture. "It's all from the twisted mind of your daughter."

"Don't look directly at me when you say that," Ed said. "Only half the genes are Lewis ones. I mean, there are only so many chromosomes that I'm willing to take responsibility for."

"Read it already!" cried Rache.

"All right, all right," said Leah, clearing her throat. She opened the small card that was taped to the flowered envelope. "Here goes.

"There once was a woman named Leah
Who had a very nice rear,
But as she approached two score
She thought there was more
But with this gift she has nothing to fear!

"What in the world?" Leah giggled as she opened the envelope. "Oh, my gosh! I don't believe it—a certificate for that new exercise spa. How nifty! How did you two ever think of it? Oh, dear, am I that fat?"

"No! No! But look, you get to take two guests. So will you take Nana Rose and me? Will you?"

"Sure. Oh, how neat!"

"What's an exercise spa?" asked Nana Sashie.

"Oh, it's wonderful," said Rache. "It's a place where you go and they strap you into these machines that vibrate the fat off you. And then they have these hot, hot baths with water that swirls violently around you. It's wonderful, but they have a lifeguard even though the water is not that deep because—Amy told me—it's so relaxing that at one of these places in New York a woman nearly drowned when she fell asleep in the water and slipped under."

Leah giggled raucously at this.

"Leah! Really!" Ed reprimanded.

"And listen, Mom, they have this great machine for thighs. It's like a barrel with these wooden knobs on it that rotate and beat against your fat, and then they have bikes with adjustable tension."

"This you pay for!" Nana Sashie's voice was high and piercing. "I can't believe it. This is what you're giving your mother?"

Rache nodded. "Listen, Nana Sashie, it's better than hooked potholders."

"I'll agree with that." Ed nodded. There had been a period in Rache's younger years when in order to come up with the homemade gift that parents are supposed to prefer to the store-bought ones, she had made hooked potholders for every birthday.

"I love this gift. I think it's incredibly original. I'm going to start tomorrow."

"And it's much better than yoga," offered Nana Rose. "No religious overtones."

"Religious overtones?" asked Ed.

"Yeah. Last time the teacher brought chrysanthemum blossoms to 'aid our meditation.'"

"What's so religious about chrysanthemums?"

"It's very religious, Ed, believe me. It has something to do with *their* religion."

"*Their* religion?" mused Ed.

"Look, I'm not criticizing. I just feel that exercise should be nondenominational."

"Open the next present, come on," urged Rache. "Here's Nana Sashie's." There was a flat box with a simple card on top. Leah opened the card and read silently the fragile handwriting. For Dear Leah, with love on her birthday. From Nana Sashie. Leah went over and kissed her grandmother.

"I think it's something you need, Leah. You don't have any." She said this every year, and every year it was the same gift: two white handkerchiefs with the monogram *LDL*. Leah now had thirty-four handkerchiefs in a neat pile in her drawer.

"Okay," said Rache. "Time for Daddy's."

"Now look, Leah"—Ed's gifts were always accompanied by a host of apologies—"if you don't like it, you can take it back and exchange it for something else, because there were lots of other choices and I wasn't sure if it was really you, you know, and . . ."

"Shut up already and let me open it."

"All right, but I just want you to know."

"Oh, you shouldn't have! Oh, Ed!" From the cotton-lined box Leah lifted an exquisite necklace of paper-thin hammered silver links. It was a masterpiece of silversmithing, each hand-wrought link with a slightly different shape.

"Quick! Put it on," ordered Ed. "I want to see it on you." Leah put the necklace on. The elegant silver links settled into the lovely hollows of Leah's collarbones.

"Nice," Ed said. "Very nice. The necklace is nothing without your collarbones."

"Cut the mushy stuff. We're hungry," announced Rache.

"Lovely," gasped Leah, and she gave Rache a squeeze as they walked through the doors into the dining room. The walls flickered from a myriad of candles, gleaming crystal, and polished silver on the cream-colored linen tablecloth. The dinner menu was splendid, with roast leg of lamb in a mustard coating, herbed rice, stuffed zucchini, and tomatoes provençal, which, because of the heavy garlic, were deemed too incendiary for Nana Sashie's stomach.

"You really wouldn't like it, Mama," said Nana Rose.

"Let me try just a little," Nana Sashie persisted.

"It'll be like a bomb exploding in your stomach. I mean, I really used a heavy hand with the garlic," Ed cautioned.

"Yeah, Nana, I saw him. I mean, there's about a clove of garlic on each tomato."

"If a child can eat it, I can eat it."

Rache made a face at this.

"Well, I just don't think it's wise," Ed said gently.

"Look," said Nana Sashie, "you won't let me eat sweets and now you won't let me eat garlic. I love garlic. I once slept in a field of garlic!" Nervous glances were shot around the table. "And that was before Maalox!" Everyone except Rache burst out laughing.

"What's Maalox?" Rache asked.

"What's Maalox!" gasped Leah. "You've lived in this house for thirteen years and you don't know what Maalox is?"

"Maalox is to this house what bourbon is to Congress!" offered Ed.

"There's a bottle in every cupboard!"

"Oh, you mean that white stuff for 'acid indigestion'?"

"I still want the tomatoes provençal!" Nana Sashie spoke in the same stubborn voice of a child.

"Okay, okay," said Leah. "Give her a small piece."

"All right," sighed Ed, and he cut the tomato. "One intestinal outrage coming up."

Nana Sashie took a bite. "Hmmmmmm, good. More please." She handed her plate back to Ed as she slipped the rest of the tomato in her mouth. "I think the garlic quite mild, actually." Ed gestured futilely at Leah and served her another tomato.

The cake was a sensation. Leah ran to get her Polaroid to take a picture. There was no argument with Nana Sashie over eating cake. She passed it up for one last tomato. Leah insisted that first Nana Sashie take a dose of Maalox "before this last insult to your stomach."

Ed tapped on his champagne glass. "Hear, hear." He cleared his throat. "If I may briefly distract the conversation from Nana Sashie's intestinal tract."

"Please do," whispered Nana Sashie.

"I have one last gift," continued Ed.

"Oh, Ed, enough already!"

"This is actually a gift for the whole family."

"Oooooh!" Rache, Leah, and the nanas exclaimed in unison.

"Just one minute while I get it." Ed went to the pantry and

returned with something large and fairly tall wrapped in cloth. "It was too big to wrap in paper so I just put this cloth around it." As he set it on the table he asked, "Who wants to unwrap it?"

Rache was puzzled. There were not the usual hesitations, the if-you-don't-like-it statements.

"Rache, why don't you unwrap it?"

"Well, okay," said Rache with slight apprehension. She leaned forwards and gave a light tug. The cloth fell off. There was a sharp gusty sound as each of the women sucked in her breath in shock. Then silence. A samovar—polished and bright —stood before them. Rache heard Nana Sashie whisper something in Yiddish. The top piece—the crown, Ida's crown— flickered unquenchably in the candlelight. The good soldier was back! Rache sat stunned as conversation bubbled up around her.

"It's a samovar!"

Even the babies liked a glass of tea from the samovar.

"Ed, however did you do it?"

From my bed I could see the samovar.

"Well, the part that Rache found started me off."

"Were you here that day?"

Like a polished good soldier.

The words floated back to Rache through the din.

"So I started hunting in antique shops and got some leads from the museum—you know, just to find the other brass parts."

Its brass catching the glow of the gas lamp in the street outside.

"I'll tell you who was really incredibly helpful and who did most of the rebuilding when we got the parts was . . ."

I used to pretend it was a good soldier . . .

"Bo Andersen of Andersen's Jewelry. You know, the son, the kid . . ."

"You mean the one who's about forty?"

"Yes. Well, he just loved working on this."

"Nana Sashie?" Leah suddenly looked worried. "Ed, I hope this doesn't . . . Nana Sashie, are you all right?"

A sentry in the darkness standing watch over us.

There were two small pockets of loud silence in the happy din —one was Nana Sashie, whose face seemed lost in a gentle reverie, and the other was Rache, who, now over her initial astonishment, felt a confusing mixture of emotions. When she had first discovered the samovar part, Rache had been disgusted by Leah's and Nana Rose's ignorance of Sashie's Russia. But now she felt a real apprehension, as if the gulf between the two worlds had closed too quickly and the one world that she had explored with Sashie would no longer be just theirs alone. Sashie! Funny, she had never thought of her as just Sashie before. She had always been Nana Sashie. It was odd. Odder still was her father. Did he know about the meetings with Nana Sashie? Had he seen her go into Nana's room that night?

"Rache! Come back to the world of the living. Thank you."

"Oh, sorry!"

"Nana Sashie asked you a question."

"Oh! What? What Nana?"

"Would you kindly fetch the toolbox. There are a few bolts that need tightening if we are going to use this for making tea —which we are!"

After tightening several bolts, Nana Sashie declared the samovar fit for a trial run and insisted that they bring it to her bedroom.

"I don't like the idea of her sleeping with that thing burning in her room," said Nana Rose to Ed and Leah.

"What do you mean? I slept with 'that thing' burning every night in my room for my first nine years!"

"Sparks could fly."

"No, it's very well designed," said Ed. "It's probably safer than our electric toaster."

"Well, I don't like the idea."

"Well, I do," Nana Sashie said bluntly.

"I thought it was supposed to be for the whole family?" Nana Rose persisted.

"It is. You can come up to my room for tea any time. It's easier for you to come upstairs than for me to come down."

That seemed to settle it; the samovar went to Nana Sashie's room. If people wanted a cup of tea, they had to go to her bedroom, which consequently became quite socially active.

❖ ❖ ❖ ❖ ❖ ❖ ❖ **XV** ❖ ❖ ❖ ❖ ❖ ❖ ❖

BUT that first night the samovar would belong to Nana Sashie and Rache alone. At least, that was the thought in Rache's mind as she moved across the hall carpeting to Sashie's room. It was 2:30 in the morning and Rache had not even needed the alarm to wake her for this short hike toward the long journey through time, through Nana Sashie's time, to the world that might not be strictly their preserve for much longer. She stepped into the bedroom. The polished good soldier loomed before her in the night. The street lights were lawns away in the suburbs, and yet the samovar seemed lambent and luminous, as if catching the reflections from a distant mirror.

"I knew you'd come tonight."

Rache jumped in surprise. The voice sounded so young.

"Nana Sashie!"

"Who else?"

"You're awake?"

"Yes."

"How's your stomach?"

"What about my stomach?"

"The garlic didn't upset it?"

"Of course not! Stop with the stomach already! Come sit down here beside me." She patted the covers. "Quite remarkable, isn't it? With just one piece to start with, your father did an amazing job! And now he's back, the good soldier." Nana Sashie gave Rache's hand a squeeze.

Like iron filings pulled to a magnet, Rache's and Sashie's eyes were drawn to the glow of the samovar. The old eyes flickered with new color. Time melted. A century bent. There was a young voice.

"We're going with him?"

A strange waxy face with dreadful eyes had melted out of the mist of the cobbler's alley. Sashie felt a stinging cuff on her ear as soon as she asked the question.

"Be quiet!" Her father's voice was sharp. He leaned forward and greeted Wolf warmly.

As Sashie saw her father's hand actually touch the other man's flesh, she felt her stomach turn, and she recoiled in horror. She sought her mother's hand, but Ida was like a statue, rigid, her eyes unseeing sockets. Through the fog came the disembodied cluckings of chickens. Sounds, even the strangest ones, took on a peculiar intimacy in the thickness of a fog, and Sashie shivered as she heard these.

"Wolf Levinson," said Joe. "My family—Sashie; my wife, Ida; my sister, Ghisa; and my father, Sol."

Wolf nodded and touched his hand to his hat in his first social gesture in twenty-five years.

"We have no time to waste, Joe." Sashie felt her mother wince at hearing her husband's name spoken by this man. "So if you will follow me, the wagon's right here. I have arranged the coops so you can get in and lie flat. Then I'm afraid after you're settled I must put them back to cover you."

"Yes. Yes, Wolf, we understand," said Joe.

"Well then, this way and we can lay out the bedclothes to make it more comfortable." There was a bustling as bundles were taken off backs and rearranged in the wagon. Sashie was busy untying her own, but she suddenly was aware of a stony, inexorable stillness directly behind her. It was as if Ida were not even breathing. Joe put down his toolbox and moved quickly to her side. He spoke gently. "Come on now, Ida." He began to untie her bundle quickly. "It's going to be all right."

"The chickens are one thing, but the devil is something else!"

"Don't be silly, Ida." But Ida did not answer.

Crawling down a temporary center aisle Wolf had made, Sashie was helping Ghisa spread the bedclothes on the floor of the wagon. As long as she kept helping Ghisa she did not have to look at or really think about the strange face with the awful eyes. But now there was trouble. She could sense it. Ida was not moving and Joe was desperate. Sashie peeked around a coop. Her mother's bedrock stance shocked her. She felt the real possibility that the escape might never begin, that they were doomed to stand here until morning, when they would be discovered. And then what? She had absolutely no idea how her father could ever move her mother onto the wagon. It would

take a miracle. Sashie suddenly thought of Moses standing by
the Red Sea before it parted. Next to Ida, the Red Sea was a
puddle to jump. Sashie had never seen anything as unmovable
as Ida. Partially hidden by the coop, Sashie listened to the drama
taking place between her parents.

"Ida, you must!" pleaded Joe.

"Who is this man?"

"Ida, he is our only chance."

"What hell has he been to?"

"Ida!" Joe swallowed hard and brought his face close to hers.
"For the love of our children, get in that wagon!" What in the
world was he going to do, Sashie wondered. Carry her?

"Ida, say this with me." And Joe began a soft chant: *"She'ma Y'Isoreal! Adonai Aloujanou! Adonai Echod!* Hear, O Israel! The Lord our God! The Lord is One!"

Sashie's eyes widened as she saw her mother lean on her father's arm and begin to move. As she took these first steps on the longest journey, Sashie could hear her mother whispering softly the words of the *Shema,* the Jewish statement of faith.

The blankets had been spread. Ida and Sashie stretched out in the most forward part of the wagon, each with a baby tucked in at her side. The space left between them was for Joe. At their toes were the tops of Ghisa's and Zayde Sol's heads, who were stretched out from the midsection of the wagon to the back end. Ida and Sashie settled in as best they could. With a small pillow under their heads, they had about twelve or fifteen inches clearance between their faces and the chicken coops. This seemed much more ample than Sashie had imagined. There was plenty of room to place a tier of the samovar over her face as a shield.

"This isn't bad, Mama," said Sashie, trying on the samovar face mask. "Here, try it." Sashie turned toward her mother to hand her the brass piece.

"No. I want to see," Ida said emphatically.

"So much for the samovar!" muttered Ghisa, whose voice floated up from Sashie's feet. There was no way that Sashie could see Ghisa's or Zayde Sol's face, and she found that she missed the smirk that must have punctuated her aunt's remark. She could just see her mother's face by turning her head to the side, and she could see Louie's chubby face, tucked in under her own arm and sleeping for now. Cecile's face was mostly buried under her mother's blouse, but Sashie listened hard and through the clucking gale of the chickens above could hear the deep, throaty sucking noises of the infant as she nursed, a sound she had heard a thousand times but which thrilled her in a new way. Her father had arranged himself between Ida and Sashie. His head was a little forward of theirs, so he did not block their view of each other, and in order to see Joe, Ida and Sashie needed only to crane their necks and look up a bit. He quickly put a hand on each of their shoulders.

"Well, is everything as comfortable as possible here? You know, you don't need to be on your backs; you can turn over on your stomachs. Everyone all right?" Joe asked. "Ida?"

"All right." She replied flatly.

"Sashie?"

"Fine, Papa."

"Ghisa?"

"Lovely!" Darn, Sashie thought. She wished she could see Ghisa's face.

"Papa?" Joe asked.

There was a slight pause, then, "I'm alive?"

"All ready?" Wolf's face loomed at the end of the aisle.

"All set," Joe answered. His voice seemed tinged with excitement that bordered more on joy than fear.

"All right, I'll put on the last coops."

There was a great clatter and clacking as Joe dropped the first coop into the center aisle where it rested on the edges of the flanking coops. A little chunk of white night disappeared, and Sashie felt her heart beat faster. More clatter and clucks, and another piece of the night vanished. One by one the coops were dropped, and piece by piece the world above Sashie and her family was eaten up. The clucking of chickens choked the air around her, and Sashie found herself gulping for breath. Terrified of inhaling one of the white feathers that tumbled crazily through the air, she tried to screen her mouth with her scarf, but then it was harder to breath.

"Sashie!" Her father's voice came through strong and gentle. "Look at me, Sashela." She craned her neck towards her father. "You breathe like me now. Do just what I do. First in through the nose, not too deep, then out through the mouth blowing softly. Slowly. Take your time, Sashela. There's plenty of air. And you think of nice things, like the smell of bread baking and kites flying and the first leaves of May and lighting Hanukkah candles."

"Harruh!" They heard Wolf grunt and slap the reins on the horse's back. The wagon groaned and lurched forwards, the wheels creaking, and they were on their way. Sashie thought she could count every cobblestone as the wagon rolled down the cobbler's alley. But she kept breathing just as her father had told her to and tried to think of nice things—things that now seemed rare and wondrous, like an open window on a starry summer night, a raindrop's path on glass, April branches with leaves curled tight as babies' fists.

They must be on Vaskeyevka Street. She would try and guess their route as they went. But she certainly could not see, and at this hour there were no sounds except the blizzard of cluckings that raged inches above them. She wondered if they would go by the park. And then after the park, what? She had never gone beyond the park. The Alexandra Gate of the park was the farthest perimeter of her life. Some chicken droppings splattered on her cheek, but just as disgust welled up inside Sashie a new noise split the cluckings—iron spikes hitting stone. The world above was laced with the rhythmic strikes.

"Whoa! Whoa!" She felt the wagon stop. Ghisa slid forwards a bit, her head pressing on Sashie's feet, and Sashie's head pressed against her father's arm. Louie's eyes flew open. Sashie opened her eyes as wide as she could and, staring directly into the little boy's, commanded his silence with an unblinking and fierce gaze that was intended to freeze his tongue. Quickly she reached up her sleeve for a sugar stick and popped it into his mouth. It worked, this time. Outside she could hear Wolf conversing in Russian with some men. The street was being repaired and impassable for a four-wheel vehicle. They must turn around and take Zolodievka Street. There followed a great deal of jangling and jolting shot through with Wolf's grunts and barks at the horse. Sashie felt the wagon roll backwards a few feet, then forwards. There were more barks. From the noise Sashie thought that Wolf must be off the wagon and guiding the horse around by pushing and pulling on the harness. Louie cried out once, but the sound was drowned by the tumult of the horse whinnying in protest, chickens clucking, harness jangling, wheels creaking, not to mention the string of curses and barks emanating from Wolf.

"Old man!" said one of the street workers jovially. "Watch your tongue. You know there are not just roosters aboard your wagon. I see some hens!"

The swirl of feathers seemed to freeze in the air above Sashie.

She felt Ghisa grab her foot and her father's hand bite into her shoulder.

"Just joking!" She heard the man protest innocently. "Can't you take a joke, old man?"

Sashie had not heard Wolf say anything to the street worker, but she had a sense that Wolf need not say much to fill another with dread. The wagon was finally turned around. The street worker stood just by Sashie's side of the wagon now. With only the boards between them, she could hear him mutter nervously to the other, "Queer eyes!" Sashie could feel Wolf climbing into the driver's seat.

"Harruh!" he yelled. The wagon lurched forwards and clattered out of the street.

If they had to take Zolodievka Street instead of this one, it must be fairly near, and if it were fairly near, reasoned Sashie, the Alexandra Gate of the park was not that far away. Approaching the edge of her known world, Sashie felt a ripple of excitement run through her body. She remembered suddenly a book her father had shown her that had a picture of a map from long long ago, from before Columbus had discovered the new world. The map showed a world with the continents and oceans known in the early fifteenth century. At a certain distance from the land, sea serpents were drawn riding through the crests of waves, with the legend HERE BEGINNETH THE REGION OF THE DRAGONS. Except, thought Sashie, in Russia the dragons live everywhere, and she and her family were supposed to be escaping from them to the tsarless region of what angels? She was not sure. Although she herself had not dealt directly with the dragons, Sashie never once doubted their existence. One did not have to have tea with the tsar and tsarina to have his life sabotaged by them, or their ministers, or the notorious Black Hundreds, who were nothing but street thugs glorified by the tsar and given a license to kill Jews. She remembered her father's stories of the army and she had the feeling that that was not the half of it. And she would never forget the night the news came of her grandparents. She had been only three years old at the time, but she would never forget it—the hollow, stunned voice of her mother repeating over and over, "Both of them?" No, Sashie believed in these dragons, and something deep, deep inside told her that the dragon's fire had scorched Wolf. His eyes were queer because he had looked straight down the fiery throat. She wondered what it was he had seen. She would probably never know, Sashie thought, and she could certainly never ask.

Louie had finished his sugar stick and was demanding more. Sashie felt the wagon turn another corner. They must be near the Alexandra Gate. Had Columbus been forced to begin the region of the dragons with a baby wailing for more and twisting his nose, as Louie was now twisting Sashie's? "Hush, hush!" commanded everyone, but Louie would not be quiet.

"Give him another one!" hissed Ghisa from Sashie's feet. Sashie groped up her sleeve for another sugar stick. "Here," she huffed, "what do I care if you grow up to have rotten teeth!"

Ida prayed a strange prayer—that her baby boy would grow old enough to have rotten teeth. And Joe, buoyed by Sashie's relentless optimism, smiled quietly to himself and patted his daughter on the shoulder.

Sashie had fifteen sugar sticks. At this rate, she calculated, they would not last the day. "We might need the b-o-t-t-l-e." Ida and Joe were not overjoyed at the prospect of drugging babies, but such a possibility had had to be planned for on this trip and a bottle of milk with a light sleeping draught had been prepared. Just then Sashie heard a torrent of water from a slop bucket being thrown out a high window. The chickens on the left side of the wagon forward of her sent up a loud cackle. They must have caught some of it, and then under the layer of cackles was another noise—a steamy hiss of curses from Ghisa. There seemed to be more street noises now—shutters being opened, dogs barking, more wheels creaking, fragments of early morning talk drifting out of doorways as shopkeepers readied for trade. But where were they? It sounded nothing like the noises one would hear around the Alexandra Gate. There were not any buildings near the gate from whose windows slop buckets would be emptied. They must be beyond the gate and near the out-skirts of Nikolayev, Sashie thought. As if to answer her question, there was suddenly a new sound and a new motion as the wheels of the wagon rolled from cobblestones to wood. The bass tones of the wooden planks rumbled beneath the wheels and the rush of coursing spring waters muted the manic cluckings. Even Louie, who had managed to sit up, stopped sucking on his sugar stick.

"What dat?" the baby demanded softly.

"It's the river." Sashie whispered. "We're leaving Nikolayev now."

"Oh."

"Be a good boy, Louie!" Sashie patted his knee. Louie was

now starting to crawl around, exploring under the chicken coops. It seemed to keep him quiet and drain off some of his energy, so nobody tried to stop him. There wasn't far he could go.

As the wagon moved from the bridge to the dirt road, the clucks and cackles rolled up once more in a suffocating swarm. Oh, to hear water again! thought Sashie. But the liquid resonance of the flowing river was soon a memory obliterated by the cackles that seemed to bristle right inside Sashie's brain. She would go mad if she listened to the chickens another minute! She would think of a song. But she could not think of one. She would try to hear the road under the wheels. But she could not hear it. The road did, however, feel different from the cobblestone streets. It was softer. The speed seemed slower—not just slower, but *thicker*, Sashie thought. How can motion feel thick? It was not a bad feeling. And the noise, it wasn't noise. She caught herself. How can I hear noise, Sashie thought, above the cackles? But she did. And it was different. It wasn't noise that was reflected from hard surfaces like cobblestones, wood, and granite. It came from a deep quiet center. They were soft and sucking sounds; the sound of things being absorbed, soaked up. It's mud sounds, thought Sashie, ecstatically. "I am listening to spring mud." It was like beautiful music to Sashie.

Just above the mud but not as high as the wagon top she heard another sound. It was the whispering of a south wind blowing through winter grass. Sashie had never in her life been outside the city. She had never known the sound of the vast quietness of the country, which absorbed noise to make new sound. She lay perfectly still, listening as the country sounds bloomed around her like huge flowers.

Through the minutes and in and out of hours they slept, whispered, ate a hunk of bread or piece of potato. The babies were doing tolerably well and the sleeping draught had not yet been needed. A huge baked potato kept Louie busy for twenty minutes. A medley of whispered nursery rhymes delivered by Sashie and her father averted a near tantrum.

Sashie had just finished drawing tiny faces on both her thumb and index finger for a puppet finger show to entertain Louie when she felt Wolf slow the horse.

"Whoa!" he said.

The horse and the wagon stopped. Just as Wolf had begun to speak to the horse, Sashie had heard distant rapid beats, like small explosions in the earth.

"Trouble!" Wolf's voice was tight with fear. "Everybody must be quiet! It's soldiers." He paused, and Sashie thought she could hear the breath catch in his throat. "My God, it's an imperial regiment!"

Then there was a timpani of cold metal as sabers and spurs jangled in the air. Sashie had managed to grab Louie and press him flat on the floor. Her father lay his leg over the little boy's kicking ones and Sashie clapped her hand over his mouth.

"Hail! In the name of their imperial majesties, the Tsar Nicholas and the Tsarina Alexandra!"

Wolf mumbled something conciliatory, but Sashie could not hear the exact words, for the only noise was that of metal clanging, leather squeaking, hooves striking the ground, animals panting, and occasional coughs. The chickens' clucking was eclipsed by the noises that accompanied the tsar's regiment of twenty on an exercise in the countryside. And beneath the chicken coops the human cargo lay in frozen terror.

"You carry chickens, I see . . ." The commander spoke. "And where are you bound for?"

"Oh, just to Borisov to deliver them for my boss to a client."

"How generous of your boss. I am sure he would not begrudge a few chickens for the tsar's regiment, and the client will never miss them."

"Lieutenant, if you please, two or three coops." Sashie heard a man jump from a horse.

"Aaaaagggg!" screamed Wolf. "Hold it!"

" 'Hold it!' You old Zhidi!" The last word hung in the air like a dagger dripping blood. "Zhidi," the abusive word for "Jew," had become quite popular with the latest wave of pogroms. Sashie trembled all over. She pressed her hand harder on Louie's mouth.

The commander spoke slowly. "You deny one of the tsar's most loyal and favored regiments a few chickens? To deny the tsar's officers is to deny the tsar, and to deny the tsar is to deny God!" the voice thundered.

"No! No! I do not deny anything to you, your . . . your excellency. It's just that the coops are in bad repair and if you carry them with you they are bound to come apart and the chickens escape. Better you take the chickens slaughtered."

"Fine. Lieutenant, skewer a few chickens then, if you will."

There was a bright flash and Sashie's breath suddenly locked in her throat. Her eyes widened in terror as she saw the tip of a thin silver blade slice through the mesh and come within three inches of her face. Time stopped as her eyes focused on the glinting sliver of death that played above her. She could even see the scarlet sleeve of the officer's jacket. The three gold buttons blazed through a small flurry of white feathers, and the black decorative braid at the cuff was like four coiled snakes ready to strike. The silvery death dance went on raging above her face and throat. The moist still air from her half-open mouth fogged the blade tip.

"Here! I find you a fat one. Those are all skinny." The blade stilled. The silver death retreated through the slashed mesh to the world above, and Sashie fainted.

A few seconds later she came to and heard Wolf talking rapidly.

"Those are the scrawny ones. Good breeders, but no good eating. Now over here we have your scratchers."

"Scratchers?" asked the commander.

"Yeah, scratchers. They have to scratch for their food. Makes 'em tough. Stringy. They're big chickens, mind you. Weighty, but quite tough. No flavor. But here. Here in the middle we have our plumpsters—we call them plumpsters." Wolf prattled on faster than a runaway cart down Kliminsky Street on the science and technology of poultry. "With the plumpsters you get more meat per cubic centimeter than any other kind of chicken. Succulent! Juicy! You see, the plumpsters are not required to scratch for their food. And what food it is! Whole-grain bread soaked in gravy, pumpkin seeds, kasha. We Zhidi should only eat like that! The plumpsters main job in life is eating, with an occasional stroll in a very small area. A chicken, one might say, truly fit for a tsar. Please sire, your sword. I will fetch you the plumpest of the plumpsters. Yes, a rare bird indeed!"

Sashie felt the wagon shake as Wolf pulled himself up on the side. "Kosher is quick!" She heard Wolf mutter to himself in Yiddish. In less than three minutes he had slaughtered ten chickens. Blood dripped down the center aisle onto the bed-clothes.

"Your chickens, your excellency. May you and your officers eat them in good health!"

"Your client will never miss them," came the reply.

As the spurs dug into flanks, whinnies mixed with leathery squeaks and metallic janglings filled the air. The command finally came—"Forward!"—and then the rapid explosive noises of eighty hooves striking the earth as they moved off with their imperial load.

Zhidi, Sashie thought, when at last she could think again. Wolf called himself a Zhidi. How very strange that he could do this—abuse himself with this foul word even though it was done to ingratiate himself with the commander. For the first hours after the encounter with the regiment, Sashie lay in a state of total exhaustion. It was as if her nerves, her brain, and each muscle in her body had used every bit of energy available. Gradually, however, she began to realize that she was alive. It was a miracle. It was as if she were a newborn baby with an older mind that could appreciate the wonder of its own birth—of being born a whole, complete human being. She tingled all over with the sheer excitement of her own living body. She touched her throat and face. She traced the gullies and curves of her ears. She pressed hard through all the layers of clothing and felt a rib. She took a joyous inventory of her body. Then after the miracle of survival was confirmed, she thought of Wolf and the word he had used in reference to himself. How absolutely confounding and unfathomable it was. She could not imagine ever calling herself by this horrible name, no matter what the danger was.

Sashie had stared unblinkingly as Death sliced the air just inches from her face and throat. She was sure Wolf had seen something worse, but what was it? The haunted man contained a death riddle. Sashie had been brought to the edge, but Wolf in some way had crossed over.

The fog had long ago burned off and slants of sunlight had

pierced through the mesh and feather storm into the nether-world of the coops. But now the sun was at too low an angle to light the wagon, and Sashie felt a twilight chill. If she could only move more, she would feel warmer. Louie was warm as a puppy from crawling around under the coops, and though he was now sleeping, his short little body could curl up into a nice ball perfect for conserving energy. Sashie tucked him in closer to her own body to steal a little heat. Soon she drifted in and out of a troubled sleep that jolted and lurched and flashed with silver blades dripping blood. Then everything stopped and she woke up into a night-still world with her own hand fast at her throat.

"All right!" Wolf shouted. She felt him jump down from the driver's seat. "We're here."

"My God!"

"Thank God!"

"Am I dead or alive?"

"Or a chicken!"

"It's all right, Ida, we're here!"

"Oh, Joe!"

"Hang on, folks. I'll get the coops off in half a second." Sashie felt Wolf climb on the back end of the wagon. She heard the clatter of the first coop being removed.

"Ah!" exclaimed Ghisa with wonder as she saw the first piece of the world above. Another two coops were removed and Sashie heard Zayde Sol recite a *broche*, a prayer, upon seeing the evening again. Then another coop was removed and a square of night sky reappeared, black velvet chinked with stars. Piece by piece the sky came back and the wind, with the smell of winter grass and earth, blew across Sashie's face.

Each person had to be helped off the wagon by Wolf and, except for Louie, walked around a few feet by him until their legs and back regained their strength. Sashie needed Wolf's arm only for a couple of steps. Almost immediately she was off on her own trying out her new legs. First she tried walking a few meters, but the night was so warm, the air so gentle, and the field so vast that Sashie felt she must dance, leap, fly through this startling country. Under the starry dome of the Russian night Sashie whirled and jumped. Her head thrown back, she watched the stars spin and smelled the thawing earth and listened to the wind songs in the grass.

Ghisa too was soon running and skipping in jerky little circles around a moonlit tree stump. The babies squealed and Ida and Joe said soft prayers of thanksgiving and laughed gently with each other in the night. And Zayde Sol said more *broches*— *broches* for seeing stars again, *broches* for seeing the moon, *broches* for seeing a baby walk, and *broches* for seeing a granddaughter dance.

Sashie had wandered to the field's edge to where the forest met the grass. When she came back her mother noticed a strange look on her face.

"What's wrong? You look like you've seen a ghost. You're not feeling well. You want to throw up?"

"No, no. I'm fine. I just . . ."

"Where have you been?"

"Over there . . . by the trees." Wolf was just coming across from the same direction.

"Well, what's wrong?"

"Nothing I just . . ."

"Well?" persisted Ida.

"There was a dead squirrel, that's all. I guess it died over the winter. It just surprised me, that's all."

"Well, this is the country, *bubeleh*. You see things you're not used to seeing. Things are different here," said Ida, hugging her daughter. "But we're here and we're all alive!"

"All alive!" whispered Sashie.

"Joe," Wolf said as he climbed up into the seat of his wagon, "your wagon will be here by dawn. The fellow's name is Reuven. He won't want money. He enjoys the risk of stealing from the high mucky-mucks—a bit of a firebrand, you know."

"Wolf!" Joe reached up and took both the man's hands in his own. "You have . . ." Tears welled in Joe's eyes and something caught in his throat, so he swallowed and began again. "Until my dying day I shall remember you as the man who risked his life to help our family become free."

The rest of the family came to stand near the man who had helped them. Even the babies were still. "Wolf," continued Joe, "you are no firebrand. You are our Mordecai!"

✻ ✻ ✻ ✻ ✻ ✻ ✻ **XVI** ✻ ✻ ✻ ✻ ✻ ✻ ✻

SASHIE watched Wolf leave. She made herself watch him all the way as he drove the wagon down the road, silver in the moonlight. She would watch his broad back and hunched shoul-

ders until the wagon disappeared over the road's first hump. And then she would turn and never forget.

"Forget what?" interrupted Rachel. Nana Sashie's eyes opened a bit wider as if in slight alarm. Her pupils were dilated in the dim light of the bedroom as she studied the young, unimaginably young face of her great-granddaughter. It could have been her own face eighty years ago.

"Never forget Wolf, of course!" she snapped.

"Well, the way you said it I thought you meant something more."

Nana Sashie's eyes narrowed as she looked at Rache. So clever and so young, she thought. Too young for that. Too young! Then quickly she said, "Nothing more. There's nothing more." And the old woman's mouth settled into a firm tight line as if to clamp her tongue.

"Want a cup of tea, Nana?" Rache said, feeling a tension that needed to be broken.

"You mean a glass of tea," corrected Nana Sashie. "Yes, that would be lovely."

Rache quietly poured the tea into two glasses set in brass holders.

"How much water, Nana?"

"Ummm, about one centimeter for me and about three for you." Nana Sashie had never switched off the metric system after arriving in America, which to Rache simply proved that if you wait long enough, things come full circle. However, she herself was less than fluent in the metric system, and in the dark it was exceedingly confounding. She turned the spigot key and tried to guess when the liquid in the glass had risen a centimeter. "Here," Rache said handing the glass to Nana Sashie. "Hope this is all right."

"Ummmm, not bad," said Nana Sashie.

Rache giggled. "That sounds like something Joe would say." Nana Sashie beamed with sudden warmth. "You're right, Rache! It sounds just like something Papa would say. You're getting to know them, aren't you?" Rache nodded. "We didn't have any tea out in the field that night," Nana Sashie began suddenly. "Funny, with all those samovar parts and everything. But we had left the teapot behind. It was not nearly as fine as the rest." Nana Sashie nodded towards the good soldier, its luster engulfing the night around them.

"Didn't you get cold?" asked Rache.

"We built a fire for the night, and by early morning, when it began to die, Rev had come!" The old eyes became magnificently alive with a twinkle unlike any Rache had ever seen.

"Room service!" he cried, and his voice was swallowed up in the vastness of the dawn countryside. Sashie and her family arose bewildered and stiff-jointed as the lithe, powerfully built young man jumped off the wagon and danced up to them carrying a pot. "Quick, start the fire again! I brought you soup."

"Do you have a firebrand?" Sashie asked quietly, her voice full of wonder. The man paused just as a dancer might, but his body still seemed full of the music, and his deep-blue eyes crinkled at the corners as they lighted on Sashie.

"Say that again, child."

"Do you have a firebrand? Wolf said you were a firebrand."

The man threw back his head and laughed at the sky. "Yes! I am a firebrand. I bring you chicken soup and revolution!"

"You are Reuven?" Joe stepped up to shake his hand.

"Yes, Reuven Bloom at your service."

Sashie thought it was the most beautiful name she had ever heard. There was nothing harsh about it. Yet it was strong. Strong rivers flowing gently, that's what it sounded like to her. His face was dark and ruddy from the outdoors. He must spend all his time stealing wagons and driving them around the countryside, Sashie thought. His face had creases beyond his years, but they were creases from squinting at the sun and laughing at the sky. In light, quick movements Reuven put the pot on the fire and began to stir. While he was stirring the soup Sashie sidled up to Ghisa. "What's a firebrand?" she asked. Ghisa too was transfixed by the man and stared unabashedly. Neither Ghisa nor Sashie had ever seen a person move with such grace and freedom. It was as if he had never known the containment of a room or even the tight narrow streets of a village. His movements, although never grand or sweeping, had a fluid ease and strength that matched the landscape, that belonged to the rivers and mountains and plains.

"Well, what is it?" Sashie asked again.

"What's what?" Ghisa asked vaguely.

"A firebrand!"

"Oh, it's a revolutionary. You know what that is." Sashie did not know. She had heard the word a lot lately, but she was not really sure what it meant. Was it a radical like Mismatch? This man was no Mismatch.

"What do you mean, a revolutionary? Is it something musical?"

"Musical?" Ghisa was perplexed. "No. You know, it's someone who stirs things up, inflames people with ideas, tries to turn things upside down to make things better politically." Sashie did not really hear the political part. She heard what she knew to be the ultimate truth about this man—he was a stirrer of feelings, of deep human feelings. She did not feel inflamed. She felt moved deep down inside.

Reuven was now serving the soup in little bowls that he had fetched from the wagon. First he had dipped a bowl of soup for Ida and one for Ghisa. Then he came with one for Sashie, who was sitting on a rock near the fire. As he bent over he spoke cheerfully. "Even firebrands like me still believe in serving the ladies first. Here you go!" Sashie looked straight up into his face and peered at him with an intensity that even startled Reuven Bloom. "You're no firebrand, Mr. Bloom. You are filled with music!"

Reuven was astounded. "Who . . . how do you know that?"

"I just know it."

He looked at her as if he were seeing something of infinite rareness. "Just . . . just stay right there. No, I mean, get up and serve the rest of the soup while I fetch something from the wagon." When he returned he had a violin under his arm. Standing by Sashie, he put his foot on the corner of the rock where she sat, tucked the violin under his chin, raised his bow, and began to play. At first there was a slow procession of notes stirring the air, so unearthly that Sashie looked to see if there were really human fingers drawing the bow and playing the strings of the violin. They listened as the air around them thrilled to the sounds. Sashie thought that if butterflies sang, this is the music they would make. Then Reuven played music that was so hushed and fragile that Sashie thought of a world so silent that you could hear the sounds of flowers moving in the breeze, and these sounds were the ones that Reuven played. Sometimes it seemed as if the wind alone moved the strings of the violin. But it was all as passionate as the man himself.

Sashie had had to force herself to watch Wolf go, but she could not keep herself from watching Reuven Bloom as he stood in the road playing his violin when she and her family drove off in the new wagon. It seemed as if the music alone, rather than the horse, were moving their wagon as they rolled away from the solitary figure in the road. Sashie watched and listened to Reuven as the noble music seemed to envelop her very soul. And although their paths diverged now, she knew it was not always to be so.

They had reversed their clothes before starting off that morning, and now in the regalia of the Purim costumes they seemed wrapped in the festive spirit of the holiday. The sun shone, and the horse, a vigorous old soul, was quite obedient to the unpracticed, though sensitive, hands of Joe on the reins. Reuven had given him a brief lesson in driving, and Joe had taken to it immediately. Sometimes when the horse slowed to a steady walk, Sashie would jump out of the wagon and skip ahead. She would gather handfuls of dried grasses and plants and husks of things gone by and make bouquets and garlands with Ghisa in the back of the wagon while they rode along. "I never knew,"

said Sashie, as she braided together some light and dark stems, "that there could be so many different shades of brown."

Ghisa snorted cheerfully. "It takes a trip to the country to tell a ten-year-old girl what she never knew!"

Sashie settled back on a soft pile of bed clothes and looked at the sky. She thought about the shades of brown and then she thought about the music of Reuven and his violin. Every note, every phrase she could remember. The small apartment on Kreshchatik Street seemed so far away.

CHEV 2 KILOMETERS, the sign read. The road curled like a ribbon down into the valley where Chev nestled. They passed occasional stucco houses that stood close to the ground, their thatched roofs like stocking caps pulled down low over the brow. Sashie liked the easy order of these small farms, each with its house and barn nestled in the center of the property and its fences following the gentle slope of the hills. There were no sharp angles. There was no hard-line precision. Everything was hand-built to accommodate nature and the contours of the earth.

"Well, St. Petersburg it's not!" Ghisa muttered as they rode through the tiny village. Sashie had no idea what St. Petersburg was like, but this village was fine with her. It looked just like something she would draw with her wax pencils—a jumble of wobbly geometry: square buildings, tall rectangular ones, curved façades with pointy roofs, gently sloping roofs, conical ones. A wood wagon's delivery to some houses halted traffic for a few minutes, but to Sashie's delight it was right in front of a bakery shop that specialized in Ukranian breads. In the window was a myriad of different breads and sweet buns—doughnut puffs, almond horns, sweet dough coils, rolls and rings and loaf cakes and breads shaped into roses, balls, crowns, horns, knots, and shells.

"Sashela! Your eyes are as big as a *polianitsa!*" Ida said.

"A what?"

"That one, three in from the left," Ida said, pointing at the window to a white puffy disk of bread at least two feet around and topped with a crusty cap. Ida knew all of the names of the different kinds of breads. "There's *pampushkey,*" she said pointing, "*bulochky, palochky, zavyvanets, rohalyky, solomka, bublyky.*" Linked together, the bread names made a wonderful poem. Just as Sashie was whispering their names and enjoying the bubbly sounds on her tongue and lips, the baker ran out.

"*Prosymo zavitaty!* Welcome! Where are you bound—Nimsk? Where are you from?"

"Borisov," Joe responded quickly.

"Ah, you go for your Purim play. Yes, yes, I hear about those. I went to one once. Hard trip from Borisov? No! No! The mud isn't bad this year."

The baker was one of those jovial sorts who was so talkative that he managed to answer most of his own questions. "Ah, you have babies!" he exclaimed, chucking Louie under the chin. "You a good boy? Of course you are. Here, let me run in and get you something." When he returned he held a *polianitsa* in one hand and a brown-paper bundle in the other. He handed the large loaf to Ida and the paper bundle to Sashie. "Don't eat it all in one afternoon." He patted her hand and winked. "But you can peek." Joe and Ida thanked the baker warmly. " 'Tis nothing. 'Tis nothing," he repeated.

Sashie opened a corner of the bundle to peek in. There were several bulky, hard ring-shaped rolls, three *rizhoks*, or horn buns, and several *solomka*, sweetened bread in the shape of straws. She was fiercely tempted to try a *solomka*, but Ghisa, as if reading her mind, interrupted her thoughts. "Wait at least until we reach the edge of town." Sashie looked up at Ghisa. "Come on, Sashie, it won't be long. As I said, this isn't St. Petersburg." And in another hundred meters they had passed the last building in the tiny town of Chev.

"Now?" said Sashie looking again at Ghisa.

"Now," said Ghisa, and she put out her hand for a *solomka*. Sashie gave one of the bread sticks to Ghisa, then one to each of the rest of the family.

The road curled up from the valley floor and the wagon wheels creaked as Joe guided the horse around tight bends and curves. There was one point where the road was so narrow and the drop-off so steep that everyone got out of the wagon and walked while Joe led the horse by his bridle. But then the road straightened as it pierced a darkly magnificent forest, dense with majestic trees and occasional shafts of sunlight.

On the rocks and at the base of trees there grew something that looked soft and green. Sashie had never seen it before but it looked just like velvet. Her father told her that it was moss, and more than anything Sashie wanted to get off the wagon and pick some, or at least touch it. But her father was reluctant to stop in the middle of the forest in the dwindling light of the afternoon.

"Sashie, we can't stop. It's getting late. What do you think this is, a botanical expedition?"

"It'll only take a minute. I just want a little piece."

"I know your little pieces. You'll be there all afternoon patting the stuff."

"No, I won't. What's a botanical expedition, anyway?"

"Not what we're doing."

"Well, what is it?"

"It's a trip whose purpose is to gather samples of plants," Joe said with great exasperation.

"You mean it's educational?" Sashie asked, putting special emphasis on the last word.

"Stop bothering Papa! How can he drive with all this?" scolded Ida.

"I'm not bothering him. I was just asking if botanical expeditions were educational."

"Educational shmeducational! It's not the purpose of this trip. So you'll just have to be ignorant. . . . Eat a *solomka*."

"They're all gone," said Sashie.

"All gone!" chorused Ida and Ghisa.

"I want a piece of moss," Sashie whined.

"You know," said Joe turning around to face Sashie, "for such a smart girl you can really act like a complete baby!" Sashie started crying. Then as if it were contagious, Louie and Cecile joined in.

"Oh, for God's sake. Stop the wagon!" cried Ghisa. Joe stopped the wagon. "All right," Ghisa ordered, "out of the wagon! Find your darn moss. You have twenty-five seconds. I'll count."

Sashie scrambled down from the wagon and headed for the thick carpeting spread at the base of a tree. She fell down on her hands and knees onto the spongy damp moss. "Eight . . . nine . . . ten . . ." Ghisa's voice rang out in the deep silence of the forest. Sashie had never felt anything quite like it— velvety and furry. "Thirteen . . . fourteen . . . fifteen . . ." She burrowed her fingers into its softly bristling greenness. "Seventeen . . . eighteen . . ." It was amazing how easily the moss, great fragments of it, could be torn away. "Twenty . . . twenty-one . . ." She could see the little damp rootlings that hung severed from the earth on the underside, and the dark bare spot in the ground like an open wound where the patch had been torn away. It was like peeling flesh from the earth. Sashie's hands suddenly froze. Then very quickly she took the patch she had torn out and carefully fit it back into the raw bare spot, patting it gently. "Twenty-four . . . twenty-five . . ." You could never tell it had been removed. "Back in the wagon!"

"I'm here!" shouted Sashie with a wide grin as she swung her legs over the edge.

"Where's the moss?" asked Ghisa.

"Over there. I really just wanted to touch it, that's all."

"And that's all!" Ghisa scowled. "All that for a little moss pawing . . ."

"Come on, let's go." Joe slapped the reins on the horse's back. "No more educational stops."

They heard them before they saw them. The road had just come out of the forest and swung into a deep bend that obscured their vision, but there was the sound of several hooves striking the earth and then the awful familiarity of the jangling metallic noise. Sashie's hand went immediately to her throat. She saw her father's back stiffen.

"*Stop* in the name of their imperial majesties, the Tsar Nicholas and the Tsarina Alexandra!"

"Oh, God!" whispered Ghisa, and she clutched Sashie's hand.

The captain's horse with a shock of white blazing its face danced nervously. "Where are you bound for?" the captain demanded. The retinue was a small one, not more than six or seven men.

"To Nimsk. Just down the road a piece."

"I know where Nimsk is," the captain said acidly. "Where are you from? Chev?" Sashie found the horse's blazed face oddly distracting. It gave the animal a wild, uncontrolled appearance. "And why," continued the captain, "are you . . . you," he gestured at them, "dressed in this manner?"

"Oh," said Joe quickly. "We are going to Nimsk for the Purim plays. We are players. My wife here is the queen, the old man the king." Sol touched his crown lightly and smiled. "I am a courtier." No use going into detail with these louts. "My sister, a lady-in-waiting, my daughter—"

"Well," interrupted the captain, "take your play to Nimsk, but don't bother to go on to L'Bov," he added darkly. There were snickers from the other soldiers. "You won't find much of

an audience there." A coarse laugh came from a fellow with a lumpy red nose who whispered something about "Zhids." The blazed white face of the horse tossed impatiently. "On your way. You should make it to Nimsk by dark," the captain said, drawing up his reins and spurring the horse.

That night they camped a few miles beyond Nimsk in a thin grove of trees in the middle of a field of garlic. There was a strong, though not unpleasant, odor. A stream ran down a hillside right through the grove and out into the field again with the coldest, most wonderful water Sashie had ever tasted. The sun was just going down beyond some distant mountains, and the sky was streaked with blue-gray clouds nearly the same color as the mountains. But just between the mountain tops and the underside of the dark clouds were islands of peach-colored clouds. Then there were short gray clouds that Sashie imagined to be dolphins swimming among the island clouds. For a few brief seconds the sun on its downwards slip sprayed its light through the island archipelago and drenched the dark mountains in the most glorious rose color. Then the rose seeped out and a cold purple stole over the mountains.

"Sashie! Come over here by the fire. You'll freeze, *bubeleh!*"

"Just a minute, Mama!" Just another minute to savor alone the changing colors of a spring twilight. Sashie watched the long shadows of the mountains slide across the field. This was all so new to Sashie, being outside, watching the sky, feeling the texture of the earth—being apart! It came to her suddenly like a tiny explosion in her brain—being apart, not alone, just apart. In the miniscule apartment on Kreshchatik Street Sashie had never been farther than twenty feet from any of her family.

When she went outside the apartment into the street, she always went with an adult, who usually held her hand. When she went to another apartment to play, there were still people around, close around. But here, here she was apart, maybe one hundred meters or more apart. She looked across and saw her family's dark shapes moving slowly around the fire, preparing for night. All were absorbed in their tasks; her father feeding the horse some hay that Reuven had put in the wagon, her mother boiling some diapers in a watering pail over the fire, Ghisa slicing bread for sandwiches, Zayde Sol saying an evening *broche* for the setting sun. They are all over there, Sashie thought. I am here, apart. She stopped for a second in her thoughts. Though I love them just the same, this is fine.

"Sashie! Come on!"

"Coming!" she shouted, and skipped across the one hundred meters just as the purple shadows enveloped the campsite and chased the last of daylight away.

The sky pricked out with a thousand stars, and the moon rolled up round and shimmering, silvering the grass and the trees with its light. Sashie stayed awake star-watching and imagining flying off into the velvet night sky to touch the bright star points. She had touched moss that day for the first time, and she had seen trees bigger than she ever believed existed, and she had found at least twenty shades of brown and woven them into a garland, and she had seen a sky turn like a bruise from pink to purple, and she had heard the deep green stillness at the heart of the forest, and she had heard the most beautiful music a human being could make. Her last thought as she fell to sleep was of Reuven Bloom and what music would he make for this starry night. She could almost hear it, and then she was asleep.

The sounds were very small and muffled, the ones that woke her up, and for several minutes she could not tell exactly where they were coming from. But then she felt something jerk on the blanket beside her and hiccup. Ghisa! She thought, Ghisa is crying.

"Ghisa! Ghisa!" she whispered, "what's wrong?"

"Nothing."

"You're crying."

"So what?"

"So, why are you crying?"

"Can't a person cry in private?"

"What's wrong, Ghisa?" Sashie said pleadingly, and shook her shoulder. "Turn around and talk to me."

"What's the use!" Ghisa moaned and rolled over. Her face was pale and streaked with tears. Her nose and eyes were red.

"You look awful!"

"Thanks."

"What's wrong? Why are you crying?"

"Look, you might love this country life, but I miss things terribly." There was a muffled sob.

"You mean, like Mismatch?"

"Well, yes, him," Ghisa answered hesitantly, as if that was not all that she missed. "And Zev," she added.

"The one with the cigarette?"

"Yes, he's the one . . . and Isaac."

"The handsome one with the limp?"

"Yes, that's him. And Shlomo."

"The one who speaks French and smells a little?"

"Ahh!" sighed Ghisa, as if savoring the aroma of Shlomo, "yes."

"Gee, Ghisa, I didn't know that you had so many boyfriends. I thought you said you never wanted to marry?"

"Who said anything about marriage! I miss them all, the whole club, Nikolayev. I'm a city girl." She sighed again.

Sashie suddenly remembered the counting book in which Ghisa had sewn the miniature scenes of Nikolayev. She reached up her sleeve and pulled it out. "Here!" she announced. "It's not the real thing, but it might help."

Ghisa sucked in her breath sharply. "Sashie! You brought this! This is the thing no larger than a full-grown roaster that you chose to bring from home." Sashie nodded silently. "But Sashie, you outgrew this book years ago!"

"So? It's still beautiful."

"Oh, Sashela!" Sashie felt her eyes fill. This was the first time Ghisa, (Ghisa! of all people!) had called her Sashela.

"You want to know what I brought?" Ghisa giggled.

"What?"

Ghisa raised herself on her elbows and rummaged in a scarf which she had tied up in a bundle. She drew out a small folding sewing kit made of felt and untied it. On top of the neatly arranged needles and swatches with buttons and thread pinned to them was a metal frame with a small tintype picture.

"It's me!" gasped Sashie.

"Umm, hmmm," nodded Ghisa.

"Me at the park and one half of Mismatch and some of you!" A blur appeared on the left edge of the picture frame that vaguely resembled half of a man in half of a hat, the rest of

which seemed to have stepped out of the frame. On the right side of the picture was a third of Ghisa, who must have moved when the shutter closed.

"You remember the day?" Ghisa asked.

"Of course. But why did you bring this picture? I'm the only one in focus."

"I know. Maybe it's significant. But it was such a lovely day. Remember? So even out of focus it all comes back, and besides, when you grow old, to be an old old lady in another country, you'll be able to say to your children and your grandchildren and your great-grandchildren, 'I was born in Nikolayev'!"

"I was born in Nikolayev." Sashie repeated the simple words, and they became full of mystery as she imagined herself speaking them to her children and her grandchildren and her great-grandchildren.

❖ ❖ ❖ ❖ ❖ ❖ XVII ❖ ❖ ❖ ❖ ❖ ❖

THEY stopped for lunch the next day on the high part of the road by a grassy knoll that looked over meadows and fields below. Sashie, enjoying her new-found solitude in the country, climbed to a higher rocky promontory that gave a view of the deep curve that the road took as it wound down from the high part. Looking back, she could see from the promontory that another road joined with the one they had been traveling, making a *Y* with their road right at the point below where she was standing. When she looked again, she caught her breath as scarlet coats and glittering metal emerged out of a smear of dust that rose from the second road, and like a glaring beacon in the middle of the tumult was the blazed white face of a horse. With horror Sashie realized what was coming towards her. For one awful moment she was paralyzed; she could not move or think or breathe. Then her wits returned and she raced like a spirit down the rocky steep side of the promontory. A thorn rammed into her palm but she did not feel it. Her cheek was scraped bloody as she cascaded down a sheer drop of granite on her stomach. She had just one thought: to reach her family and warn them. What ever could they do? Hide? Bury the wagon? Climb trees? The most ludicrous thoughts began to stampede her mind.

"Mama! Papa!" The family looked up and gasped at the sight of Sashie, blood-streaked and smudged with dirt, her eyes wild with fear. "It's the soldiers from yesterday—Nimsk! The ones we saw!" She was so out of breath and gripped with terror she could hardly speak complete sentences. "Yesterday's soldiers! They're coming! On the other road! Over there!"

Joe grasped the whole situation immediately. His eyes became cold, his voice taut. "Don't panic. Do just what I say. Everybody reverse your clothing, dark side out. We're going to a funeral. Pop, you're the corpse. Stretch out flat in the wagon and try not to breathe when we go past them. Ghisa, Ida, Sashie, wrap your babushkas so they can't see your faces. Keep your eyes down. Ghisa, let me borrow your glasses, it will help disguise my face better and they won't remember you as well."

Everybody worked with amazing speed and efficiency and just as they began to roll, the soldiers appeared. "*Stop* in the name of their imperial majesties, the Tsar Nicholas and the Tsarina Alexandra!"

They stopped and the captain began to speak again. "My good people, yours is a mission of sadness." Immediately from the captain's tone Sashie knew that they were not recognized, nor even thought to be Jews.

"Ah, yes, sire, our father has died and we are taking him to the family burial ground in Blevka." Just at that moment Ida and Ghisa began to weep noisily. The babies as always joined in the crying and Sashie threw in a sob or two herself.

"Be on your way then. May the spirit of our Lord be with you." Then of all things the captain made the sign of the cross over the wagon. Ghisa choked in a kind of startled embarrassment. Ida crossed her eyes in disbelief, Joe blanched, and Sashie just prayed that Zayde Sol would not rise from the dead and throttle the captain. But they were rolling vigorously down the road before any such action could occur. When they were clearly out of sight and sound of the soldiers, the corners of Joe's mouth began to turn up in a smile, and the harder he tried to press his lips into a straight line, the more the corners curled. Ida looked at him out of the side of her eye and a laugh bubbled up in her; then another. This was all Joe needed. He soon was laughing so hard that he could hardly drive. But the horse seemed to do fine and trotted on with its cargo of laughing people.

The first signs they had of something strange were the thin black whisps of smoke that curled languidly into a placid sky. "A fire of some sort, I guess," said Joe. "Maybe a farmer's hay barn." But as they drove on, the smell became sharp, biting the air with an acrid insistency. Zayde Sol was becoming visibly upset, as if old smoldering embers in his memory were being stirred into a new fire.

"We must turn off this road, Joe. This road is no good."

"There's no turn-off, Pop. This is the only road."

And then like some diabolic hand a sign appeared just ahead with an arrow: L'BOV 3 KILOMETERS. It was not the sign that caused Ghisa and Sashie both at the same moment to let out the terrible heart-scratching screams. Draped obscenely over a stake that was driven into the post was the disemboweled body of a cat, its mouth, all teeth bared, was pulled back in a mock echo of Ghisa's and Sashie's screams.

"Sashie! Ghisa! Take the babies and lie flat on the wagon floor until I tell you to get up. Ida, shut your eyes." Joe ordered.

But Ida looked at him defiantly. "You think shutting my eyes will help!" she said under her breath. "So this is what they did to L'Bov."

There was no need for Zayde Sol to shut his eyes. He was wrapped in a blizzard of prayers, chanting and rocking back and forth in a kind of hypnotic fury that had at its center a calm, blind eye that had seen it all and could see no more. But Sashie and Ghisa peeked between the slats of the wagon. And through the cracks and holes of the boards, the fragments of total destruction appeared like scraps from the apocalypse—a charred cart with a blackened hand reaching stiffly out; a cow bloated in death, its pointy hooves faintly absurd as they stuck straight up into the sky; burned-out cottages, their windows like blind eye sockets; a large star of David, once fastened to a prayer-house door, lay scorched in a pile of rubble. The only sound was the soft hiss of the still-smoldering fires.

Joe began to chant in a low voice the *Kaddish*, the prayer for mourning, slow and heavy, but imbedded at the very center of his voice was a wail so human in its frailty and noble in its dignity that Sashie's eyes stung with fierce tears.

Their course had departed with that of the river soon after noon on the first day of their journey and they had not seen it since, but Joe had said that when they saw it again they would know that they were nearing their destination, for the same Bug River that ran through Nikolayev also crossed the border. Sashie was the first to hear the low, hollow roar of the coursing water. "I hear something!" she said suddenly. Her eyes widened. "I hear water!" And then, "Papa! The river!" She was now balancing on the back of the driver's seat with her hands on her father's shoulders and looking over his head. She had just caught a glimpse of a straight narrow section of the river that was white with rushing water.

"*Ai-yee!*" A joyous cheer rose from Joe, and the somber mood that had wrapped the wagon and the family like a dark shroud since L'Bov seemed to lift. Even the old horse trotted on with renewed vigor. The growing roar of the tumbling waters was a cheerful rondo that urged them all on. When they arrived at the

river bank, Joe halted the wagon. They all got out and instinctively walked to the edge of the river, Joe holding Louie and Ida holding Cecile. They all dipped their hands into the water to rinse away the grime of the day's journey. They took off their shoes and pulled off their stockings and let the bone-achingly cold water run over their feet. Sashie sat on a rock and dangled her feet in the vortex of a swirling eddy. It was frigid—so cold that it ached right up to her knees and pains shot through her thighs, but she did not mind. There was life in the strong river rhythms and she wanted to be part of it. For the first time all day she thought of Reuven Bloom.

Nobody had to say anything, but when it came time to climb back into the wagon, they all reversed their clothing so that the costume side was showing once more. For a brief moment Sashie wondered which side was the real one—player or mourner. They each had a unique reality, but they had also fused with one another in a confounding way. From then on, the road followed the river.

❖ ❖ ❖ ❖ ❖ ❖ **XVIII** ❖ ❖ ❖ ❖ ❖ ❖

THEY had remained in a small grove of trees several hundred meters from the border. The glow from the sentry house was visible, and occasionally a few terse words from a sentry could be heard. The night was brittle with cold, the stars sharp in the sky. Sashie sat in the wagon wrapped in a blanket. She felt as if every fiber of her body and brain had been drawn into a thin silver wire, taut and keen. Her face was quick like a fawn's. She had shoved back her babushka so she could hear every sound of the night. Her eyes were so used to the darkness that they did not need to strain to see every flutter of the smallest leaf. At precisely one minute before midnight Joe stepped out of the trees. A minute and a half later Sashie heard footsteps coming across the ground towards her father.

"You got the gold?" a thick voice growled.

"Yes." Joe replied. "In the wagon."

"Let's see it." Joe and the guard returned to the wagon.

"Ida, the money for the gentleman."

Ida was sitting wrapped in a blanket with Sashie in the back of the wagon. She took the samovar bottom and held the bowl up for the sentry to see. "Sir," she said. Her voice was remarkably even. "We have taken the precaution of baking the gold pieces into cookies."

"Okay, let's see these cookies," the man said warily. How rude, Sashie thought, that he did not even have the courtesy to address her mother as madame. Ida bit into one of the cookies. Sashie could hear her teeth strike the gold.

"Here," Ida said and handed him a gold piece.

He did not change his expression. He just said one word, "Another!" Ida obeyed. Again Sashie heard the gold click of her mother's teeth on the coin. Again her mother handed the sentry the gold piece.

"Another!" he ordered.

This could go on all night, Sashie thought.

Then the man said, "Let me pick it."

"Fine," said Ida. "Here from underneath the napkin, those are the gold ones in the bottom layer. The plain ones are on top." The sentry dug into the samovar and picked one. He bit it and struck the coin. The taste of gold seemed to lubricate his spirits. "You are a clever cook, madame, and unfortunately, since I find myself without a container . . ." There was an evil look in his eye. Sashie felt her breath turn cold in her throat and a black feeling in the pit of her stomach.

"I shall take your samovar bowl here, but in payment leave you with these plain cookies." Sashie could see that her mother was numb. The samovar was being stolen and there was nothing to be done. Once more Sashie had that feeling she had experienced months before in the apartment of seeing her brain at work and observing the silvery glints and flashes of ideas connecting.

"Maybe," Sashie said suddenly, "you should take some without the gold in case your friends back at the sentry house want some." He had his hands on the samovar and was already removing the top layer of the plain cookies and was handing them to Ida, who let them drop in her lap. "Here, let's put these on top." Sashie began to stuff a few handfuls into the napkin he had taken from the samovar. "That's the divider, so you'll know. . . . Here, put them on top of that. See, if your friends at the guardhouse want a cookie, they'll pick the plain ones first. The rest of the plain ones for us." She took a handful and dumped them in Ida's lap. "Now, underneath the napkin will be the gold." She picked one up and bit the gold. It flashed in her hand and she put it beneath the napkin. She herself was now totally confused, though the sentry seemed pleased by her efforts. "My

clever child, what a shame you're a Zhid!" Just then they heard some more footsteps coming toward the grove. "Hurry up!" he barked. Sashie's fingers and hands, lost in a blur of speed, worked as fast as the wings of a hummingbird hovering to gather nectar.

"Here!" She shoved the samovar bowl into this hands. The sentry turned to leave.

Joe grabbed him by the throat. "Get us across," he said through clenched teeth.

"All right!" he rasped. He waited a few seconds and listened. The footsteps were going in another direction. A feminine laugh was heard in another part of the grove, then the metallic noise of a sword scabbard being unbuckled and dropped to the ground. He put his fingers to his lips and motioned for Joe to take the horse and lead it by the bridle. It was a short distance on a well-worn path. Within two minutes the family had left Russia forever.

<hr>

❖ ❖ ❖ ❖ ❖ ❖ XIX ❖ ❖ ❖ ❖ ❖ ❖

THE table was a perfect oval, and the faces seemed to Sashie like perfect circles of happiness. Many had the plump, dimpled roundness of Ida's, as if the pleasing contours of Ida's beaming face had radiated out like ripples in a still pond. Next to Ida was her twin brother, Samuel, and between Samuel and his wife, Bathshepa, were their twin daughters, Gittel and Sheyntse, and then their teenage son, Mendel, and Zayde Benjamin, Bathshepa's father, and his wife, Menye, and next to her Zayde Sol, and then gorgeous Sarah, the eldest daughter, in whom all the plump roundness had been elongated into a lovely oval face with high cheekbones and just a wink of a dimple. Next to Sarah was Ghisa and then Joe and then back to Sashie.

There had been toasts all evening, and Sashie was feeling drowsy from all the wine, even though Joe had been judiciously diluting her glass with water. But he was not about to breathe a word of caution to her. Indeed, he poured a little more wine into her glass and then his own and rose to make a final toast as the sweets, the hamantaschen, were brought in. Holding a glass of wine in one hand and a hamantasch in the other, Joe began to speak. "And now for the sweetest toast of the evening and the year." Sashie squirmed, a little embarrassed over the obvious humor. "To all of us, not just here at this table but all over the world, who love freedom, for we are the best lovers! Blessed be the freedom lovers! *L'Chaim!*" Joe raised his glass to drink and then took a bite of cookie. Just as Uncle Samuel was saying, "Next year Jerusalem!" Sashie saw the gold flash in Joe's mouth as a coin dropped from his tongue. There was a stunned silence as the coin spun noisily on the plate. He reached for another cookie. Sashie heard the familiar click of gold on teeth. Ida then reached for a cookie. She bit. Another click, another flash of gold, another coin glittering on a plate. Sashie,

Ghisa, and Sol all reached for the cookies. Soon there was gold dropping from everyone's mouth.

"But I thought you said you gave him the gold ones and kept the plain ones?" Bathshepa said in a high voice.

"I thought we did." Ida replied. "I don't know."

"It's some kind of a m-m-miracle!" Samuel stammered, but just as he said the word "miracle," Joe and Ida and Ghisa and Sol's eyes swung towards Sashie.

"Sashie!" they all cried.

"I don't know," said Sashie in a wine-thick voice, "it was all so confusing; so dark; and when he wanted to take the samovar and we had to take out the plain and then put in the gold and then more plain . . ."

"To tell you the truth," Nana Sashie said to Rache on a darkening winter afternoon, "I really don't think I did know what happened."

"But you said that you wanted to stop the sentry from taking the samovar," Rache said.

"No, no," Nana Sashie corrected, and leaned out of the blizzard of shawls gently waving a finger at Rache. "I knew there was no way I could save the samovar part. I was just thankful that he hadn't noticed Mama's crown, but I was so enraged by the idea of his getting everything. So I thought there might be a chance of salvaging a few gold pieces by substituting some plain ones. Somehow the cookies just started flying. I was talking so fast, my hands were going so quickly, the night was so bitter cold, that I got thoroughly confused in the middle of the whole thing, and I really didn't know who had what by the time I shoved the samovar bowl into his hands."

"Hi, guys!" Ed knocked gently on the door. "Don't mean to intrude, but Mom says it's time for dinner."

"Well, just one second," Rache said. "Nana Sashie, is that the end of the story?"

"No." Nana Sashie gave her a curious smile. "It's just the beginning."

Ed looked thoughtfully at Rache. "I hope so," he said, and then walked over to Nana Sashie and gently picked her up in his arms to carry her downstairs.

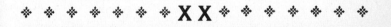

❖ ❖ ❖ ❖ ❖ ❖ ❖ **X X** ❖ ❖ ❖ ❖ ❖ ❖ ❖

N A N A Sashie died a few weeks after telling her story to Rache. She had grown quite weak several days before and had begun to refuse food. Dr. Weingard came to examine her and then told Ed and Leah and Rache, "She has decided to die, and there is not much we can do except make her comfortable."

So that's what the Lewises did. They kept the good soldier going all day and night. They took turns sleeping in her room on a cot by her bed, and they brought up the record player and put on it the stirring music conducted or played or sometimes composed by Reuven Bloom, who had been Sashie's husband for forty years.

Early one afternoon Nana Sashie slipped into a coma. Before dinner she woke up for a few brief moments. Her eyes were alert but completely colorless. She listened keenly for several seconds, possibly a minute, to a Brahms violin concerto that was playing. She looked at Rache and patted her hand quite firmly. Her lips parted in that daring half smile of an adventurer. Then she closed her eyes and died.

It was okay—that was all that Rache could remember thinking. There was sadness, deep sadness, but it was okay.

❖ ❖ ❖ ❖ **EPILOGUE** ❖ ❖ ❖ ❖

"IT'S okay to cry, Rache." I remember my mother saying that to me afterwards. I don't remember whether it was right afterwards, when we were still in Nana Sashie's room, or maybe after the funeral. In any case, I didn't cry until some time later. I think the first time was during basketball at school. Girls' basketball, at least when I was thirteen, was an exceedingly stupid sport. You could only play half the court at a time. When the ball was in the other half, you just stood around waiting for the action to come to the still half of the cavernous gym, which although drafty, managed to smell. I started crying right there, huge copious tears that splashed on to the court lines. All the girls rushed over to me, even the forwards, and when the ball finally came, there was no one to catch it. A sharp whistle blast fractured my mourning.

"What the devil's going on down here?" boomed Miss Steppenfold. The girls backed away from me. "Uh oh! An emotional crisis. What's wrong, Lewis?" I mumbled something incoherent. "You'd better go see Tompkins."

As I left the court, I heard Amy trying to explain to Miss Steppenfold, who was nice enough but a Neanderthal in emotional matters. "What are you talking about, Schwartz? Didn't her great-grandmother die months ago?"

I never went to Tompkins. I just put on my raincoat over my gym suit and took the bus to my dad's office. He canceled meetings, stopped in-coming calls, and ordered corned beef sandwiches and Cokes from a deli.

In an architectural office there's a lot of open space, several drafting tables side by side or back to back with guys in gay bow ties and women in aviator glasses chatting back and forth under skylights. So we ate in Dad's private office, the place he tells clients that the project is going over budget or won't be finished on time. I cried a lot more.

"Feel better?" Dad said when I finally stopped. I looked up at Dad. The next thing he said was exactly what I had expected. "It's just the beginning, isn't it?"

"Yeah," I answered.

"Now you can begin, can't you. I don't mean right this moment."

Dad didn't even know the whole story, but he knew me, and he knew the meaning in a strange way of being old old. And most important, he knew it wasn't history. It was family. There was no confusion.

I'm a slow beginner. That conversation in his office was

almost six years ago. A lot has happened in those six years. Amy not only gave what I reviewed as a "refreshingly forthright" performance as Ado Annie, but managed to finish high school in three years, flash through college in two and a half, and has just started medical school. I, at a somewhat more leisurely pace, finished high school and one year of college, which is a big improvement over high school—no cheerleaders, a minimum of guidance counselors, no drama requirements, and lots of elective courses. But it has taken me a long time to get geared up to tell Nana Sashie's story. I made little stabs at it here and there along the way. I did a lot of digging around for several years and finally discovered how Sashie and Reuven Bloom got together after parting ten years before on that Russian country road. But that's another story. It was not until a year ago that I really began to grow into this story. It happened, or started to happen, on my eighteenth birthday. Nana Sashie had been dead for five years, but my mom and dad had a letter to be opened on the day of my birthday. Although it had the key to a tragic riddle, I had to laugh at Nana Sashie's style as I read it then, and re-read it now. She wrote as if there had been no interruption in the narrative, even though five years were to have passed before I could open it. She plunged right in, with no introductory frills.

Dear Rache,

Remember when Wolf left us on that country road and I said that I would never forget and tried to leave it at that, but you pressed and I evaded? You were too young for the whole horrid tale. I was too young too at the time, but I was such a curious little monster that I just inadvertently stumbled upon it. But now you're old enough to know.

That first night after we got out from under the chickens and were so joyous to be alive and breathing the fresh air and Ghisa and I were dancing around like two nuts under the sky, do you remember how I told you that I wandered to the field's edge, to where the forest met the grass? I did not tell you everything I saw. It was there under a poplar tree stripped bare of its leaves that I discovered Wolf's awful secret. I found him standing under the tree transfixed, his eyes looking down at the ground. I knew I should not approach, but I did. I had some ghastly desire to know the worst. There near his feet on a rock were the lifeless broken bodies of a mother and two baby squirrels. They were not mangled and there was really not a mark on them but their little limbs were twisted at such awful angles and their skulls caved in. Some unspeakable terror had scared them from their nests. I don't know what, but they had fallen and there was no father squirrel. I was just about to say that when Wolf looked up and said, "The father fled."

Now you know.

LOVE,
SASHIE

It has been a year since I read that letter for the first time. I don't really know what made me decide to write down the story of Nana Sashie. But the reasons for writing seem unimportant compared to the reasons for living and the reasons for dying, which I begin now to understand as the meaning of the time itself that Nana Sashie and I spent together. During those brief months I came to realize that "time marching on" is a bore and it is the circles and deviations of time that makes time curiously alive. Nana Sashie dared to take me on a detour, and in doing so she circled back, and I too. But then sometimes I wonder, was it circling back or going forwards for us? It was time out of line, but time laced with the bright filaments of memory that in turn linked two people at the opposite ends of life for a vital moment in each one's existence.